"Turnabout is fair play. What are your dreams for the future?"

Garrett's future dreams stood next to him. He could see himself as Verity's husband, a father to her children, enjoying simple evenings like this New Year's Eve. But he didn't dare say those hopes aloud.

He put it in broader terms. "I want the same things most men want. To make a difference. To build something lasting. A family. Love. Pretty ordinary stuff."

Silvery flecks sparkled in her eyes when he mentioned family and love. He didn't dare say any more. Not now, not here where her children could overhear every word.

Award-winning author and speaker **Darlene Franklin** lives in Oklahoma near her son's family. Darlene loves music, needlework, reading and reality TV. She has more than twenty books published. She's a member of American Christian Fiction Writers and Oklahoma City Christian Fiction Writers. You can find Darlene online at darlenefranklinwrites.blogspot.com and facebook.com/darlene.franklin.3.

Books by Darlene Franklin

Love Inspired Heartsong Presents

Hidden Dreams
Golden Dreams
Homefront Dreams
Saving Felicity
Small-Town Bachelor

DARLENE FRANKLIN

Small-Town Bachelor

HEARTSONG
PRESENTS

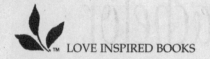

LOVE INSPIRED BOOKS

Recycling programs for this product may not exist in your area.

ISBN-13: 978-0-373-48786-8

Small-Town Bachelor

Copyright © 2015 by Darlene Franklin

www.Harlequin.com

Printed in U.S.A.

For the son of man came to seek and to save the lost.
—*Luke* 19:10

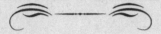

Thank you to NancyJo Andrews
who allowed me to use her name for one of
my characters. Thanks to the many who helped my son
and me through his difficult teen years.

Chapter 1

Verity Clark was running late. Again. Her cell rang just as she grabbed the day's mail. Tucking the flyers under her left arm, she hunted in her purse for her cell. When she finally found it, she dropped both the mail and the phone on the ground. By the time she picked it all up, the ringing stopped.

For long months, her heart had raced every time she heard her phone. But now with her youngest child cancer free, Verity could relax.

She didn't recognize the acronym on the caller ID. She listened to the message. "Mrs. Clark, this is Garrett Sawtelle. I'm calling from the Chittenden County truancy office. Please give me a call as soon as possible."

Although Garrett Sawtelle was a distant cousin, their paths didn't cross all that often. She hadn't seen him since a family auction over a year ago. Her finger poised over the return-call key while she debated whether to call back immediately or later, after she had entered the stack of patient records into her home computer. Delaying would mean she might not complete her day's work on time, but the nagging worry about another looming problem drove her to call the school back first.

"Mrs. Clark, thanks for calling back."

Mrs. Clark? Garrett's formal greeting increased her concern.

"Before I get to my reason for calling, let me thank you again for selling me Clara Farley Tuttle's school bell. I keep it here in the office, and it's a great conversation starter."

Garrett had bailed out Verity when she couldn't pay for the bell after winning it at auction. "The bell looked pretty on my shelf but all it did was collect dust. Except for the time I accidentally knocked it over, and the clanging woke our neighbors."

Garrett chuckled. "I'll keep that in mind if someone falls asleep at a meeting." His voice turned sober. "How is Mason doing?"

As the town's truant officer, Garrett had worked with her the spring before last when Mason's many absences threatened to hold him back. "The doctor has pronounced him cancer free, although he will still need regular check-ups." She counted his absences on her fingers. Two doctor appointments to follow up Mason's progress. Another day, he hadn't felt well, and she'd kept him home.

"But I'm not calling about Mason."

Verity's heart beat so fast that she could feel the rush of blood through her veins.

"Are you aware that Keenan has already missed five days of school since September?"

Keenan had skipped school? Five times already?

When Verity didn't answer, Garrett said, "In addition to five complete days, he has skipped over half of his American history classes and several hours of French."

How had Verity missed the signs of Keenan's behavior? When had he become so devious? "I ask why he never brings books home. He says he finishes his homework during study hall. His grades aren't great, but after everything we've gone through the past few years, I decided I could live with it." On many evenings, she had accepted his one-word answers without question, afraid of what she might hear if she probed too deeply. *Forgive me.* Whether she was directing her plea for forgiveness to God or to Keenan, she didn't know.

"We need a plan of action to nip Keenan's absences in the bud before he goes too far. I can fit you in at eight tomorrow."

Verity couldn't bear the thought of waiting another day. "Can I see you right now?"

Garrett hesitated. "Keenan needs to come with you."

He was missing today. And Verity didn't have a clue where he had gone.

"Do you know where he might be?"

"No." The words came out as a whisper, so she cleared her throat and repeated her answer. "I'll look for him today. We'll be there tomorrow morning."

Verity was about to end the call when he spoke again. "And, Verity? I'm sorry about what's happening. Know that I am praying for you and your family."

"Thank you." After they disconnected, Verity stuck a note on her calendar: "8:00 a.m. Keenan." The fifteen-minute conversation had changed her priorities for the day. She stuffed the data entry forms back into the box. Work would have to wait, even if it meant falling behind.

* * *

While waiting for the Clarks to arrive the next morning, Garrett buried his face in his hands. Every family notification tore a chunk out of his heart. Some parents didn't seem worried. When that happened, he felt bad for the child as well as the parents.

Other times, parents did the best they could and their kids still fell into trouble. Single parents had it the worst. Sometimes, no matter how hard they worked and how much help they received, the family still broke apart. His first case had set the trend.

Garrett met Thomas Taylor when he volunteered as a big brother. The gap-toothed first grader had shown so much promise, but he went the way of his older brothers, receiving a prison sentence as a present on his eighteenth birthday.

Few cases had gone as wrong as Thomas's, but few had gone well, either. Garrett hated to see Verity Clark and Keenan heading down the same road. *Lord, help me make a difference with the Clarks. Restore my faith that I can help people instead of hurting them.*

On the way by, he touched the school bell. Verity had impressed him when she called him about buying the school bell that had once belonged to their common ancestor, Clara Farley Tuttle. After her marriage to Constable Daniel Tuttle, Clara had founded the Maple Notch Female Seminary in 1865 and had pioneered the cause of women's education in Vermont. He ran his fingers over the rough surface. The bell reminded him of his family's long-time commitment to education in Maple Notch and beyond. He played a different role than the pioneers of old, but he felt just as called.

Garrett wondered where Verity worked now that she no longer helped at her sister Felicity's tea shop. He would like to offer to meet closer to her place of business so she would lose as little work time as possible. But the authority projected by his office would put more fear into Keenan.

Having settled that question, Garrett looked over his next project. This early in the school year, he didn't have many truancy cases to work on. He did have a fairly full calendar in juvenile court, on behalf of his own clients as well as an expert witness. When he had time, he developed programs to keep kids in school. He tapped his pen on the blotter. He needed new material. The curriculum the state supplied this year struck him as boring. How could he spice it up so that kids would internalize the message?

If their behavior could change. The doubt plagued him more each year. He shoved the pages back into the file as his assistant knocked on his door. "The Clarks are here to see you now."

Through the crack in the door, he spotted two dark heads, one taller than the other. Keenan had grown since Garrett had last seen him. One reason for hope: Keenan had made it to the meeting. When parents couldn't get their kids to come, they faced a steeper uphill battle.

Garrett invited them to take a seat. Did the families have any idea how much he learned about them before they even said hello? Verity sat in the chair closest to his desk, back straight and proper, and patted the seat of the chair next to her. Shaking his head, Keenan chose the chair the farthest from the desk, pushed it to the corner by the window and rocked it back on the hind legs.

"Legs down, please." Garrett's polite tone could be deceptive, but most kids responded to his authority. He played tackle in college football and he could still take down boys half his age.

The chair legs hit the floor.

"Keenan," Verity said.

He shrugged as if he didn't care about the meeting one way or the other and stared at the floor as if it contained the answers to the world's problems.

In spite of Keenan's uninterested stance, he wasn't wearing earbuds. Garrett turned his attention to his mother. "Mrs. Clark."

Verity's eyebrows rose when he called her by her formal name. Later he might explain. He came into this meeting as the truant officer, and not as a family friend. "I have prepared a list of the dates and classes that Keenan has skipped so far this year." He pushed the paper across the desk to Verity.

Keenan didn't flicker an eyelash.

The report scared most parents. It was supposed to. Verity might figure out that the list detailed each class of each day missed on a separate line. One day's absence took eight lines. A second report added any other classes missed. Keenan's report ran onto a third page.

Verity read the list, sucking her lips over her teeth more and more. At last she looked up. "This doesn't give me a complete picture. He has to do more than show up for school every day for the rest of the year. My first question is will the school impose sanctions against Keenan for his absences?"

"All that's required at this point is that I notify his guardian. After eight absences, the student is suspended from school for a week. After ten absences, he is expelled."

Keenan's head snapped up at that bit of information. When he caught Garrett looking at him, he dropped his gaze to the floor again.

Verity licked her lips. "What do you recommend?"

"We can monitor Keenan's attendance. We'll send you a daily report. If you prefer, we can contact you as soon as his absence is discovered."

"I would like that. Can you do something similar regarding his schoolwork?"

The two of them worked out a plan while Keenan pretended he was an ostrich. "I'll make sure Keenan understands the plan. I'm sorry he was so inattentive today."

If the look Keenan sent Garrett's way had been a laser beam, he would have drilled a hole through his skull. The boy understood, all right.

Garrett watched Verity walk down the hall while Keenan straggled behind her.

"Do you think they'll make it, boss?" his assistant, Marcia, asked, after the door shut behind them.

"I don't know." Garrett sighed. "I just don't know."

Verity Clark deserved better from life.

Verity and Keenan rode home in the car, neither one of them speaking. Her mind spun with ideas to help get her son turned around. Yesterday, she had found him by himself, kicking a soccer ball around the empty playing field at the town park, looking up now and then as if playing an unseen opponent. When she appeared, he'd climbed in the car without an excuse or explanation.

If only her husband, Curtis, was alive, things would be different. Keenan wouldn't have to share a bedroom with his little brother or babysit. For five years, Keenan had played the role of the responsible oldest child. She had pushed him even harder when Mason got sick, but what choice had she had?

Now she had to take the initiative. "You already know how disappointed I am in you. I've thought about it a lot since yesterday. For now, you are grounded. That includes computer and cell phone. You're not to go anywhere except to school, home and church."

"Like I go anyplace now," Keenan scoffed.

"Then where did you go instead of school? You haven't spent all your days on the soccer field."

Silence answered her question. Verity didn't know how she could get at the truth.

They had arrived at the high school. Verity glanced at her watch. "What time is this? Third period, I think."

He nodded glumly. If her memory served her correctly, third period was geography, which he seemed to enjoy.

She opened her door.

"I don't need you to come in with me." Keenan slammed the door behind him and took off, mounting the steps two at a time while she followed at a normal rate.

"Keenan. Stop."

He ignored her, but waited for her at the front door. She walked as quickly as she could. "Thanks."

He opened the door for her, and she thanked God for the show of common courtesy. "Mr. Sawtelle says I have to sign in at the office, or else it won't count."

By the time she finished at the school, she decided she would take an early lunch with her sisters at Felicity's tea shop. Maybe they could help her brainstorm ways to get through to Keenan.

Amity was rounding the corner on foot when Verity parked in front of the Bailey mansion. Her two sisters had never left Maple Notch, except for college. Felicity had taken on the family albatross, the Bailey mansion, and Amity became curator at the Maple Notch Historical Museum.

Verity had followed Curtis as the military sent him all over the globe—at least until he went to war. When he died, she'd lost not only her beloved husband but her escape from Maple Notch.

"Hey there." Amity trotted forward and hugged Verity before they walked into the tea shop. "You look like you've had a bad day."

Verity breathed in the delicious aromas of fresh coffee, crisp bacon and baked goods. "Maybe one of Felicity's muffins will make me feel better."

Felicity appeared on cue. "Here you are." She hugged Verity and then held her away at arm's length. Concern spread across her features. "Oh, dear. Let's place your orders so you can tell us all about it." She led them to a secluded spot.

Verity melted into her chair. "I refuse to say a word until I've drunk my first cup of tea." One cup of chamomile tea with honey later, strength returned to her bones. "I met with Garrett Sawtelle this morning."

"Garrett Sawtelle," Felicity mused. "Isn't he Nick's brother?" Nick ran an organic dairy farm that supplied the tea shop.

"They're first cousins." Of course Amity knew the exact nature of their relationship. She could practically recite their family tree back to the first settlers in the eighteenth century.

"He was at the family auction, wasn't he?" Amity asked.

Verity nodded.

"I wonder if he still plays football. He looks like it," Felicity said. Maybe she thought she had the right to make comments like that since she was happily married.

Verity didn't like to admit she wondered the same thing, so she changed the subject. "He works with the schools. Only he's not a teacher. He's the truant officer."

Felicity poured a second cup of tea for each of them. Verity broke off a piece of her brown bread muffin, a mixture of rye, ginger and raisin bread in one small package.

"Keenan has been skipping classes, cutting entire days

of school. Five days already this year. He could be expelled from school if he keeps this up."

"Oh, no." Both sisters responded in unison. Almost everyone in the family went to college, and no one had ever failed to finish high school. Make that no one she knew of. Education was a universal value in their family.

"Don't worry. Things aren't that bad. Yet." But he'd gotten away with it this long. "Curtis could correct him with a look, but I've never been that good of a disciplinarian."

Garrett Sawtelle was good father material, like Curtis had been. Too bad he hadn't married and had kids. Now, what brought that thought to her mind? Married or single made no difference in how he did his job.

Verity twisted the wedding band around her ring finger on her right hand. Marriage. She had found her one Mr. Right only to lose him too soon. No one could take his place.

Chapter 2

On Wednesday night at church, when the pastor asked for unspoken requests, Garrett raised his hand, as he did most weeks. He never shared specifics about his caseload. Tonight Keenan's case weighed heavily on his heart.

Don't fool yourself. You're more worried about Verity than Keenan. The boy's behavior was a classic "pay attention to me" ploy, and his mother was smart enough to realize it. No, Verity herself drew him in. He wanted to believe she could handle it, but so many others had failed.

When they separated into smaller groups for prayer, Garrett joined with a group of young adults. Everyone else was married, but they made him welcome, and he knew they would respect his confidence. He slid to his knees with his elbows on the pew, as if he was diving into prayer.

After prayer time, his cousin Nick caught up with him in the kitchen, where he went for a cup of coffee. "This new case seems to be weighing you down." Nick pulled out a chair for Garrett to sit.

Garrett peeked into the gym. He usually played basketball with the youth after prayer meeting, but they were still assembling. "You're right. This is one I wish had never crossed my desk."

"Single mom, teen in trouble, receiving welfare?" Nick mentioned characteristics that factored in many truancy cases.

"Single-mother part is right. The teen isn't in trouble as far as I know, except for missing school. And she has a job."

"A mild case, then."

"A small scab that could turn into an open wound if not treated promptly and properly." He bent in close to his cousin's ear. "I know you won't tell anybody else. It's Keenan Clark. Verity Finch's son."

"Oh." Nick set down his cup. "You went to high school with her, right?"

"She was a few years behind me." Garrett shook his head. "I run into former classmates a lot. Makes me wonder how my life would be different if I had married back in college."

Verity's face jumped to his mind, her short, easy-care dark hair, with strands of gray here and there. Tired blue-green eyes that he wanted to make shine like aquamarine gems, from happiness, love, joy. Footprints in the sand necklace around her neck and a wedding ring on the fourth finger of her right hand.

"Hey, Coach, are you coming?" Aaron, one of the teens who played basketball on Wednesday nights, called across the gym floor. "The kids over at Maple Notch Community Church challenged us to a game and they'll be here in a few minutes."

Nick clapped Garrett on the back. "Don't worry. I'll be praying for you. Go out there and win one for the team."

Garrett's team practiced for about ten minutes before the van from the Community Church pulled up. A familiar dark head appeared in the group—Keenan. When he saw Garrett, he hung back.

Aaron ran over and introduced himself while Garrett made his way across the floor. Good. Garrett didn't speak to Keenan individually until the groups had exchanged names, positions and insults in equal measure. When the groups separated to begin play, Garrett spoke to Keenan. "I'm glad to see you here tonight. Church is a good place to hang out."

Keenan's laugh was short. "You sound like my mom."

The door opened as he said it, and Verity appeared as if summoned by his words. "Go ahead with your team." Garrett waved hello to Verity. If he did more than wave, both youth groups might jump to conclusions and start buzzing.

The kids he worked with kept telling him he should get out more. He saw single women all the time. Divorced, widowed, never-married women with children. After the roadblocks he had observed, he sometimes wondered why anyone had children.

In spite of his reservations about the situation with Keenan, he thought Verity Clark would make a fine wife for the right man. Maybe he could play matchmaker with one of the single dads he met in his work.

Verity came in with two children—Mason, and a girl Garrett had never met. Mason bounced up and down, as if he wanted to go on the floor and play with his brother. The girl sat on the floor and buried her nose in her cell phone. What was her name? He didn't know if he had ever heard it. In his line of business, that was probably good news.

Nick joined Verity on the bleachers. Garrett felt a pang that he couldn't join them instead of coaching. He blew his whistle, and Keenan and Aaron faced each other for the tip-off.

The two teams played evenly. Keenan threw himself into the game, showing some degree of skill. Would he be interested in the school basketball team? He would have to straighten up his academic standing for that. Garrett would throw out the idea, dangle the carrot to suss out his interest.

In the end, the team from Garrett's church won. "You have to come over to our church next week. So we have home field advantage," the youth pastor from the Community Church said.

"Sure." Garrett was tempted to take him aside and tell him about Keenan's problems. But unless Verity authorized the release, or he had knowledge of immediate danger, he couldn't speak of it even to the youth leader.

By the time they finished their conversation, Verity had left. Garrett suppressed a groan. He had hoped for a moment to speak with her.

Next time. Soon—maybe tomorrow.

Verity set up her workstation the way she liked it and prepared to get busy. The high school secretary had already called to confirm Keenan's presence at homeroom. After the last period, she would receive confirmation that he attended all his classes. If he skipped a class, they would call immediately. So far that hadn't happened.

Family and friends knew better than to interrupt her work except in case of emergency. If she concentrated, she could catch up on the week's stack by the end of the day.

Five patient records and fifteen minutes later, the phone rang. Felicity was calling.

Verity grabbed the cell. "What is it? Is Aunt Anita all right?" Their elderly aunt had recently entered a nursing home and was the most likely family member to have an emergency.

"No. I had an idea about Keenan." A short pause. "I didn't think you would mind if I called."

After all the interruptions with Mason's illness, Verity should be used to it. "Not really. What is it?"

"You know that saying that if you want to get something done, you ask a busy person to do it?"

"Yes. If you're talking about Keenan, there's a long list of things he could do around here, only he's not interested."

"Of course not. You're his mother. And I know he doesn't want to work at the tea shop, not after his job here didn't work out."

"I doubt that your new husband would allow him to work for you again. Not after his poor performance last time." Verity had ignored that sign of trouble in Keenan's world along with so much else when Mason was preparing for the bone marrow transplant. "What's your idea?"

"He's in danger of failing American history, right?" Felicity asked.

"Unfortunately."

"Here is my idea—earn credits for American history while working at the Maple Notch Historical Museum. Amity has worked with several students. He might like it better than going to class. She might even be able to pay him a small wage." Felicity was obviously in love with her idea.

"Let me think." Verity stared at her calendar. The busier Keenan got, the more she had to drive him around. He could get to the museum from school easily enough, but she would have to pick him up after work. Felicity meant well, but she didn't have kids and didn't understand how complicated it could be. "You're doing your peacemaker thing again. Trying to solve everybody's problems."

"It's my gift." Felicity said it so primly that Verity imagined her with a cup of tea in her hand. "Other times, it's none of my business. I'm praying for you. God will show you what to do."

They hung up, but Felicity's advice teased Verity away from her work. Who could give her an unbiased opinion? Maybe the youth pastor at church.

Or maybe—Garrett. To keep Keenan from finding her list of questions on her desk pad, she had created a file on her computer. She switched programs and added the latest question. At the rate her file was growing, she would need to speak with Garrett before the week came to an end.

After she had typed the question, she shut it out of her mind. By eating lunch while she continued to work, she finished the last record about two minutes before Destiny, her middle schooler, came through the front door. Mason came in a minute later. The phone rang, and Verity blew a kiss at her daughter as Des answered the phone.

Verity opened the kitchen cabinet. "How does hot cocoa and cookies sound?"

"Not me. I'm not hungry." Des headed for her room with the phone.

Pangs struck Verity's heart. Her little girl had grown up when she wasn't looking. She needed to spend more time with her daughter, somehow.

"I'd love cocoa and cookies, Mom." Mason grinned.

Verity's happiness meter flew to full throttle. "What do you want? Oreo cookies or Mom's chocolate chip?"

"Chocolate chip." He grinned. "Can I have some ice cream to go with it?"

"Don't push your luck, short stuff." She fixed two cups

of cocoa and grabbed four cookies for them to share. How simple problems had seemed when Keenan was Mason's age.

Take it one moment at a time, whether bad or good. She had learned that lesson during her husband's death and Mason's illness. Enjoy these moments with Mason, giggling over hot cocoa and cookies while he showed off his decorated short story about a horse. Tuck the memory in her warm fuzzy file for when she would need to revisit her happy place. Maybe his earlier illness would lessen the trauma of puberty. Maybe, but she doubted it.

After Mason retired to his room to play with his model cars, Verity looked into Felicity's idea. Could Keenan earn class credit by working at the museum? Garrett would know.

He answered on the first ring. "Verity. How may I help you?"

Her name sounded like honey dripping on his tongue, as if he had been waiting for her call, and she soaked in the sweetness. "We've had an idea about Keenan." She explained Felicity's proposal. "Is that possible? Can he earn academic credit at his work?"

"I expect so. Let me look." Pages rustled before he came back on the phone. "I had a student who worked at the library for a similar problem with English literature. If you want me to, I'll ask the school."

"I would appreciate it. Can you meet us at the museum this afternoon or tomorrow to set things up with Amity?" *Please say yes.* Verity couldn't put her finger on why she wanted to see the truant officer again anytime soon. She hoped he wouldn't see through her trumped-up excuse. After all, they did require his approval on their plan, didn't they?

"I can be there this afternoon," Garrett said. "Before we go any further, have you talked this over with Keenan?"

A car door slammed outside her window and Verity saw Keenan stand beside the car. "I'll call you back on that in a few minutes."

Garrett closed the file on his desk, hoping tomorrow he could make contact with the client's family. Several phone calls had not elicited any response to his messages. After calling at different hours over several days, he wondered if the family had moved.

More likely, the parents didn't care. The case felt like a dead-end loss and he hadn't even started. He didn't know how many more of those he could stand before he left his job altogether.

He'd rather invest his time in a case where he might make a difference, like the Clarks. Keenan had agreed to at least talk about working at the museum. Hopefully the kid could rediscover the family nerd gene, which saw most of them graduate from college.

If Verity had anything to say about it, he would. Keenan was blessed in his mother, even though he probably didn't think so. The more Garrett saw of Verity, the more he admired her.

As Garrett left his office for the museum, the cloudy, gray sky echoed his discouragement. He hated November in Vermont, stuck between the riotous colors of autumn leaves and the coming winter white. Now and then a shaft of sunlight broke through the bare tree limbs to create lacy shadows on the ground. Otherwise, it was just gray.

Such a light bounced off a historical marker on the town square, across from the museum. After Garrett parked, he took a few minutes to read it. It spoke of the role of the local militia in the Green Mountain Boys during the Revolutionary War. Amity could probably tell which of their common ancestors had fought—and for which side. Tories had given American farmers a hard time during the war.

Garrett spotted the Clarks' car coming around the corner and trotted across the street in time to open the door. Keenan's smile asked a question, as if doubting the reason for Garrett's presence.

Walking into the museum, Garrett felt as though he had crossed the portal into another time. Electric candles flickered in sconces hung on the pine logs lining the perimeters of the room, and a cheery fire burned inside a Franklin stove in the center of the floor. Amity blended with the background, in period dress complete with a mobcap covering her blond hair, which was tied in the back with a velvet ribbon.

"Hey there, how's it going?" Amity's decidedly contemporary English broke the illusion. She hugged Verity, smiled at Keenan and shook Garrett's hand. "I saw you reading the historical marker across the way."

He nodded. "How many of our ancestors were in that militia? Do you know?"

"I can show you the Tuttle family tree, if you're interested. I've made it my job to find as many of the descendants of our first families as I can. I keep learning a lot of new things."

Keenan had wandered away, studying dioramas of battle scenes. Amity pointed to him, smiling. "Boys are drawn to the battle scenes and weapons. Girls look at the house furnishings and toys. There are a few exceptions, of course. Stay here." Picking up her skirt with one hand, she made her way across the room.

Amity joined Keenan at the display case. "Have you ever been to Fort Ticonderoga?"

Keenan nodded and Amity launched into an explanation

of the two battles of Fort Ticonderoga during the Revolutionary War. The boy said more during that five-minute conversation with his aunt than he had anytime Garrett had seen him before.

The livelier Keenan became, the more Verity appeared to relax. Good. Garrett fought the urge to chat since Verity seemed intent on listening to the conversation.

A few minutes later, Amity and Keenan shook hands and motioned for Verity and Garrett to join them. "Keenan has agreed to help me set up a display concerning Saint Albans Raid and the bank robberies we had here in Maple Notch."

"Civil War?" Garrett hazarded a guess.

"Ayuh," Keenan said.

Impressive. Maybe the boy did have a serious student gene lurking beneath his don't-care attitude, after all.

"I'm also asking him to trace his family roots back to the Revolutionary War and write a paper about major events in American history during their lifetimes."

"The family tree." Garrett shook his head. "That's a tall order."

"He can do it." Amity smiled. "He needs a challenge. And I'll ask him to find as many of the original records as possible, so he's not just copying my work."

Verity said, "The school told me that you still have to attend all day. They'll change your history class for a study hall."

Keenan shrugged. "Whatever."

Garrett puffed out his cheeks. He had to be just as tough on this kid as on everyone else. For that matter, if he had followed up on the indicators last year, they might not be in this position now.

"Ms. Adams is offering a chance to bring up your history grade. That's great. But my concern is to keep you in school. If you agree to this program at the museum, it will count the same as your hours at school. Any absences will be reported to me."

Keenan scowled.

Garrett frowned, and Verity frowned back.

Chapter 3

"So you'll be working at the museum." Verity laced her voice with a confidence she didn't feel.

"I guess." Keenan tilted his seat back and stared out the window.

Verity counted to ten. She should take comfort that so far he hadn't refused the restrictions thrown at him. Her watch beeped, reminding her it was time to pick up Mason from his grandpa's home.

Did laziness or convenience convince Verity to drive around the town square from the museum to the Bailey mansion, where Dad lived? Prudence, she decided. Driving made it easier to keep an eye on Keenan.

As she rounded the corner, her cell rang.

Bernice was calling from the doctor's office. "I have another batch of files ready."

Verity called Dad and Des to alert them to her postponed arrival, promising herself that she would find extra time to spend with Des—soon.

A few minutes later, she pulled into the parking lot by the medical office building. "Mind if I go get something to eat?" Keenan pointed to the convenience store across the street.

"Sure. Do you need money?" Verity counted the cash in her purse as she asked the question.

He shook his head and left. Verity checked her face in the rearview mirror. Her hair was a mess, as usual. Neither as curly as Felicity's hair nor as straight as Amity's, she couldn't do a lot with it. To compensate, she added a dab of lipstick, and then entered the reception area.

"Hi there! How is that boy of yours doing?" The perky receptionist greeted Verity like an old friend.

She meant Mason, of course. People always asked about Mason, even when her other children stood by her side. No wonder they felt ignored. "Mason is doing well. Thanks for asking."

The doctor's PA, Bernice, walked into the waiting room. "Mrs. Clark, may I see you for a moment?"

Her question freeze-dried the lump in the pit of Verity's stomach, making it difficult to breathe. Bernice closed the door behind them. She asked after Des and Keenan as well as Mason. Verity found herself talking about the new problems with her oldest child.

Bernice shook her head. "That's unfortunate." She pointed to the box of files. "How is the work going?"

Not well, because of the constant interruptions. But Verity didn't mention that because she hadn't missed a deadline so far. When she had quit her job at the tea shop, she thought the flexible hours of data entry would be easier to manage. The problem was, each day still only lasted twenty-four hours. "It's going okay. Working on my own schedule helps."

Bernice slipped her glasses off so they hung from a

chain around her neck. "That's good to know. However, I wanted to warn you about upcoming changes."

Verity's heart pounded. The tone of Bernice's voice suggested the changes were unwelcome.

Bernice slipped her glasses back on and looked at her computer screen as if hoping for inspiration. Sighing, she returned her attention to Verity. "The doctor has decided to accept a position with a hospital in Georgia. This office will be closing by the end of the year. I'm sorry."

Verity nodded to indicate she had heard the statement, but she couldn't think of a word to say. *Oh, Lord, why did my husband have to die? I never wanted to raise my children alone.*

God never had answered that question.

"I know this is unexpected news, and I know you depend on the income, so I wanted to forewarn you. We will need help for a few weeks, as we transition cases to other doctors, but feel free to look for another job. We'll give you an excellent reference, of course."

"Thank you for letting me know." Verity reached for the box of new files. "Is there anything else?"

Bernice shook her head. "I'm praying for you." She held the door open for Verity.

Keenan waited in the car, drinking an energy drink and munching on potato chips. She should be glad he hadn't taken up smoking. At least she didn't think he had. Along with all the other questions about where he went besides the soccer fields when he skipped school, she wondered if he hung out with a bunch of potheads and gangster wannabes. Not that Maple Notch had any official gangs.

How could she unlock Keenan's mouth for answers? The parenting classes she had attended years ago focused on problem behaviors in young children. If they discussed problems with teens, she had forgotten anything they had to say. She should look for a class on parenting teens, or maybe a group for single parents.

Keenan came to the door and took the box from her before storing it in the car. "Thanks."

He shrugged. "No problem."

Maybe this was the opening to talk she had prayed for only moments ago. Before she could say anything more, however, her phone rang. When she saw the school's phone number, she answered.

"This is Ms. Adams. You called about your son. I can see you at eleven. Does that work for you?"

"I'll be there." At least the appointment didn't require rearranging everything else in her schedule. "Where shall I meet you?" Verity put the time and date into her calendar. The busier she became, the more she depended on electronic gadgets to keep her in line.

She turned to Keenan. "That was your history teacher. We're meeting tomorrow, to work things out."

"I don't want to go to that dumb old class." Keenan's earlier helpfulness disappeared beneath his frown.

"We have to work something out. Keep an open mind, please?"

Garrett pulled up in front of a dilapidated apartment and located 1D. The doorbell didn't ring inside, so he knocked. When no one answered, he peeked through curtainless windows. The room showed no evidence of occupants.

He went to the office and the manager confirmed his suspicions. "They moved about ten days ago. Stiffed me on the month's rent." While the owner didn't invest a lot of money in the apartments, he did keep his eye on his tenants and didn't allow any drugs on the premises.

Garrett nodded. Many people dismissed truancy as unimportant. Not Garrett. If marijuana was a gateway drug, truancy was a gateway to criminal behavior. He spent almost as much time dealing with legal matters as helping his clients. Things started bad and escalated quickly. "Did the mother leave a forwarding address?"

"They never do. What I don't know, I can't tell credit collectors. Or cops." The man shrugged.

Garrett handed him one of his business cards in case the owner heard anything, but he wouldn't hold his breath. Maybe the emergency contact information or employment number on file would pan out. If any had been listed. He could nose around the school, as well, or see if any of the boy's friends would open up to him.

Some truant officers were relieved when a student crossed the line from "absent" to "missing." They closed the file after only a token effort. To Garrett, those cases were the hardest of all.

The Clark family had a lot of things in their favor. With their ties to Maple Notch, they were unlikely to uproot and move. Getting Keenan back to school instead of permanently expelled was as important as ever.

The high school came into view before long, and Garrett parked at the far end of the lot. A mural of the town square dominated the lobby, familiar words written in a banner across the top. "Students are foot soldiers in the war for our minds.—Clara Farley Tuttle." The words of his distant ancestress brought a smile to his lips.

Did Clara ever deal with truancy? He doubted it. At that point in history, girls appreciated the opportunity for further education. But people hadn't changed that much. She'd had to deal with misbehavior among the students, an occasional Anne Shirley type.

Garrett walked up the steps at double pace and pushed through the doors, nodding at the security guard on his way to the office. "One of my clients has moved. I want to check his files for any leads." He handed the secretary a slip with the student's name.

A few keystrokes later, the secretary said, "We have the basic information on a computer file. I'll send it to your email."

"Good. I'd also like the hard copies, to see if I can glean further information."

The woman let Garrett sit in a small conference room while he studied the files on his laptop. She brought him the hard copies after a few minutes.

Garrett compared the information on the computer with the information he had received. Aside from a note indicating the phone had been disconnected when the school attempted to call, he also learned that the family had three children in school. Garrett went to the door to ask the secretary to check the attendance records of the younger children.

At the door, he almost collided with a woman, and the files flew from his hands. He stared into familiar peacock-blue eyes. Verity. Close behind stood Ms. Adams, Keenan's history teacher. Her lips were pursed in a frown.

Garrett said, "Sorry about the papers."

Ms. Adams stepped over the papers, and came face-to-face with Garrett. "I reserved this room for fourth period, so I'm afraid I must ask you to leave." She crossed her arms.

"Let me grab my things and I'll be out of your hair." He picked up the papers.

"Garrett—Mr. Sawtelle—can you stay?" Verity had regained her composure. She turned to the teacher. "Mr. Sawtelle brought the problem to my attention."

Garrett slid into the chair in front of his computer, closed the top, placed the stack of papers on top and folded his hands on the table.

* * *

After Ms. Adams approved the arrangement at the museum for Keenan, Garrett left the room. Vaguely disappointed, Verity headed for the parking lot. She had nearly reached her car when footsteps pounded the pavement behind her. "Verity, wait."

Garrett loped toward her from the far end of the parking lot. She welcomed him with a smile. "Sorry about taking over your room like that."

He waved away her apologies. "Delays are the norm. I'm glad things are working out for Keenan. How is it going at home?"

"I'm all right. Has something new come up with Keenan, at school?" *I hoped you just wanted to say hello.*

"I was going to bring this with me tomorrow, but since I ran across you today—here's a list of community resources." He handed her a sheet of paper.

The single-spaced list filled both sides of the paper. "Thanks. Last night I was wondering about a single-parents group for Christians. I see one meets at your church."

Garrett nodded. "From what I hear, it's a good group. And you don't have to worry about child care. That's provided, too. We'd love to have all of you visit some time."

"I might just do that."

"Garrett!" A couple of boys jogged toward them, Aaron from the basketball game and someone else she didn't recognize.

Garrett high-fived the boys in greeting and made introductions.

"Your son played at the basketball game, at church on Wednesday night." He extended a hand. "I'm Aaron Reid."

"Church? What are you doing there?" Jordan, the boy Verity had just met, laughed.

Aaron grinned. "Staying out of trouble. You should try it some time. We play basketball every Wednesday."

Jordan didn't respond to Aaron. "So, Garrett, is Ms. Clark your new girlfriend?"

If the car hadn't held Verity's back, she might have stumbled. As it was, she pretended to search through her purse for the key ring she had attached to her wrist already.

Garrett didn't look embarrassed at all. "You know me better than that, Jordan. If she was my date, I'd find a better place to take her than the high school."

Jordan shrugged. "That's too bad. She's hot. For a Mom." The boy bowed in her direction.

"Trust me, Mrs. Clark." Aaron hung his hand on Garrett's shoulder. "Garrett is one of the good ones."

Verity took in the information, but decided to leave before she received any more matchmaking advice. A minute or so later, Garrett ran after her and opened the car door for her. "I'll see you tomorrow."

"I'm looking forward to it." Verity closed the door and started the engine.

At home, she threw herself into work, but her heart refused to forget Jordan's question. Garrett's new girlfriend? The thought made her smile.

The phone rang a couple of times. Once, a notice that advised her of Keenan's presence at school popped up. The doctor's office called, reminding her about a follow-up visit with Mason. She tucked a note on her calendar. From Des, no word. Her daughter was pulling away. She hovered on the brink of puberty, but she never talked about it except for the rather uncomfortable facts-of-life talk Verity gave her a couple of years ago.

Verity couldn't stop thinking about Garrett. Her heart had fluttered when Jordan called her Garrett's girlfriend.

What hurt her more—the kid's question, or the way Garrett immediately denied it?

And why did the difference bother her?

Stop worrying. She had to enter the same file three times to get it right. How could she make her heart relax? Time for a coffee break. When she reached for a mug in her cabinet, her fingers ran over a small, rectangular box that she had forgotten about. She pulled it out.

The box had started its life as a box of matches. Back in third grade, Keenan had converted it to a promise box for a Sunday school project. He had glued blue construction paper to the top before writing "God's Promises" in his spiky handwriting and drawing a rainbow. It reminded her of a simpler time. A dozen small cards filled the cavity, with words like *love* and *joy* written on each one.

How had she forgotten this treasure? She sat it on the table to share with the children tonight. She grabbed one—the one that read *faithfulness*—and returned to her computer.

With renewed spirits, she finished about three-quarters of the box before Des came home. She pushed the box under the desk and hugged Des. Her daughter hugged her back. "Can I help with supper?"

"I'd love that." Verity threw her dinner plans out. Forget the teenage superchefs she had seen on television. Dinner for Des meant her specially doctored Boston baked beans, corn bread made from a box and hot dogs microwaved to the popping point.

Des fixed a tasty edition of her meal, and the boys thanked her without prompting. Mason went to sleep before Verity finished reading him a single book. Keenan lounged in the corner chair, his head bobbing in time to the music flooding through his earbuds. With the two-bedroom apartment allowed by her budget, the two boys took one, and she and Des shared the other.

Des sat on the edge of her bunk, reading, as well.

"What are you reading tonight?" Verity asked.

"This one." She held up a picture book, personalized with a story about her going on a fishing trip with her father. Tears shimmered in her eyes. "I can't remember what Daddy looked like."

"Oh, honey." Verity climbed next to Des and pulled her daughter close, while both of them cried.

Later, much later, Verity eased Des on her bed and returned to the kitchen for a glass of water. Keenan had moved to the living room couch, his math book open in his lap. Verity wished she had her phone so she could sneak a picture of him busily doing homework.

He glanced up and took out the earbuds. "Mom, what's going on? Why did Jordan call you Garrett's girlfriend?"

Chapter 4

"Is Ms. Clark your new girlfriend?" Jordan's question reverberated through Garrett's mind as he waited for his toaster strudel to warm. The crust burned, and he scraped off a few flakes of the burned crust before he bit into the fruity goodness. Running three miles a day gave him an excuse for a guilty pleasure or two.

Garrett sat down with a cup of coffee and turned to the sports section of the newspaper. He established the pattern of following sports first from his dad, a lifetime Red Sox fan. November was a busy sports month, when hope abounded for the other three major league teams in Boston—the Patriots, the Celtics and the Bruins.

Since Garrett had helped Maple Notch win its sole high school football trophy, he followed the high school and college news, as well. The football season had almost ended, basketball had already started. Keenan showed promise as an athlete. If he improved his standing at school before spring, he might be interested in baseball.

In the garage, Garrett grabbed his basketball and spun it on his finger like one of the Harlem Globetrotters. Maybe he could catch a game over the weekend. He tossed the ball through the hoop on his garage wall, where it landed in a laundry basket on the floor. Laundry. Another task he put off as long as possible. Seeing Verity, playing basketball and watching football made him a lot happier than folding clothes.

If he didn't do the laundry, he'd have to wear a dirty shirt to the Clark home tomorrow. He tossed a couple of shirts in to presoak and jumped in his car.

His workday proved satisfactory. He learned that the family who had disappeared had moved in with family in the next county. He contacted the truant officer there and asked him to follow up on the student. Maybe the kid would do better. He prayed that it was so.

Laundry followed by a soup-and-sandwich meal made for a boring evening. After he threw his clothes from the washer to the dryer, he scanned his phone for a buddy to play a game of pickup basketball.

No one was interested. He had the names of a few single women, as well, but he wasn't interested in them. Verity's number stared at him, tempting him to call, but he would see her in the morning. Instead, he called his cousin Nick, who kept early hours most days because he got up early to milk the cows that were the basis of his dairy operation.

Nick didn't answer, however, and Garrett didn't bother leaving a message. Maybe he could watch *Any Given Sunday* again. Nah. The dryer buzzed and Garrett grabbed the clothes to hang them up and avoid ironing. His cell rang when he got to his bedroom, but stopped before he got the phone out.

Nick. Garrett finished hanging the shirts and called back, reaching Nick this time.

"How are you doing, cuz?" Nick said.

"Okay." Garrett knew how lame his words sounded.

"I know. The two of us, the last of Maple Notch's eligible bachelors, staying alone at home on Friday night. At least tomorrow I have curling practice—get me away from all my ladies for the day. You want to come? You know you're always welcome."

"Not tomorrow. I have other plans." Garrett smiled when he thought about seeing Verity again.

Nick missed a beat. "Plans that involve a woman, by any chance?"

"Yes—not really."

"She's either a woman or she's not," Nick teased.

"She's the mother of one of my truants." Garrett forced the words out. Verity was so much more than someone's mother.

"You like her."

Garrett didn't bother to deny it. "It gets worse."

"What? You can't be interested in the mother of one of your clients? I might think it's the only way you meet women."

"No. Well, that could be a problem. I've known her all my life, but never really noticed her before."

"Someone I know?"

The words came out of his mouth slowly. "Verity Clark. Verity Finch, you know."

"The pretty brunette who sold you the school bell?"

So Nick had noticed. "That's the one."

"When do you see her again?" Nick asked.

"Tomorrow morning."

Nick whistled. "You've got it bad."

As soon as Verity woke up on Saturday, Garrett's visit popped into her mind. Did she have time to take a hot shower, do her hair and maybe add some makeup?

No, because Saturday morning breakfast was a Clark family tradition. Before she mixed the pancake batter, she checked her latest post for her blog, about mixing work and family, before posting it.

Des popped into the kitchen. "Can I make the pancakes this morning?"

Saturday breakfasts stretched back to the days when Curtis was still alive and Keenan was a baby. When her husband was home, he cooked. A wave of loneliness washed over Verity.

"That sounds great!" Verity took advantage of her daughter's offer to enjoy a luxurious shower before slipping into jeans and her New England Patriots T-shirt, adding a dab of lipstick and tying her hair in a ponytail.

Des searched the fridge for fruit to add to the pancakes and grabbed a few apples.

Verity took a couple of apple peelers and handed one to Des. The cookbook fell open to the quick-bread page as soon as Des touched it. She assembled all the ingredients before starting.

Verity surveyed the refrigerator for herself. She used to cook breakfast every day when she worked at the tea shop. She could name a dozen different egg dishes off the top of her head, but pleasing the kids took extra thought. The apples in Des's bowl inspired an apple and ricotta cheese omelet.

High-pitched giggles announced that Mason had wakened, and a few minutes later, Keenan's bass voice added counterpoint before they came to the kitchen. He slouched onto the couch, stretching his legs across the cushions, while he picked up the TV remote. Verity tensed, ready to remind him that television watching was off-limits. After he flipped through the channels, he turned off the set and tossed the remote on the coffee table, Verity relaxed.

Omelets and pancakes were sizzling on the stove when the doorbell rang. "Keenan, will you get that?" Verity said.

Feet banged on the floor and Keenan kept his book in his hand as he walked toward the door. When he looked through the peephole, he said, "It's Mr. Sawtelle." His angry tone soured the happiness around the apartment.

Garrett had arrived early. Keenan had made a mess of the living room, and dishes were stacked in the sink. Verity took a deep breath, reminding herself that Garrett wasn't here to check her housekeeping. "I was expecting him, just not for breakfast. Invite him in."

Sliding two fingers between the pages to keep his place in the book, Keenan opened the door and took a step back. "Mom's in the kitchen." He sat back down on the couch and opened up his book again.

Verity took stock of the amount of food. The omelet was big, and Des had a stack of pancakes warming in the oven while she cooked more. There would be enough to invite Garrett to eat with the family. By the time Garrett crossed the living room, Verity had set another plate and mug on the table.

Garrett looked at the table. "I didn't mean to disrupt your breakfast."

"Don't worry. I hope you'll join us," Verity said.

Des kept her back to Garrett. Was she upset, as well as Keenan?

The pancakes finished a minute before the coffee. Verity flipped a second omelet, and they all sat down to a feast.

The children stared at Garrett, as if he were an extra-terrestrial alien. "You'll have to excuse the children. We don't have guests at breakfast very often."

"Never." Des glared at Garrett. "Not since Dad died and we had all those people coming to our house. When we had a house."

Verity flinched. Old memories died hard. Brightly, she said, "Whenever Curtis was home, we always made Saturday mornings a special family time. And after he died, well, we continued the tradition."

Keenan leveled his gaze on her, over the back of the box of cereal he was reading. "Aren't you going to ask us what our best and worst things were this week, like you usually do?"

Mason jumped up. "I forgot." He ran into the living room and opened his backpack, returning with a sheet of paper. He handed it to his mother.

She looked at the red A at the top of the page of a list of words and grinned. He had struggled with spelling all year. "Well done." A refrigerator magnet reading World's Best Mom held up last Sunday's bulletin. She tossed the bulletin in the trash and hung the spelling test next to his collage of things he was thankful for from last week's Sunday school lesson.

Garrett didn't say much, slowly devouring the stack of pancakes on his plate and draining a glass of orange juice.

"What did your English teacher think of your essay about Clarinda Quincy?" Verity asked Des. She had read the handwritten version about the mayor who had led Maple Notch through World War II. Des's interest in her locally famous great-grandmother encouraged Verity.

"I threw it away." Her daughter scowled. "I only got a C+."

Garrett snorted, and Verity glanced at him.

"When I wrote an essay, C+ was what I expected to get. I'm better at talking than writing."

"I don't believe that," Verity said.

"It's true. The reports I have to write are the bane of my existence."

Verity tore her attention back to Des. "I thought it was a great essay." She felt a spike of resentment, wanting to go to battle for her daughter.

"You couldn't see the print for all the red marks." Des shrugged. "At the bottom, she said she liked the way I told the story, but I needed to check my spelling and punctuation."

Verity's irritation peaked again, this time because Des had good grammar skills, but poor typing. Perhaps she should type the story for her next time. But no, her daughter had to learn and doing it for her wouldn't help her improve.

"You're not mad at me?" Des asked.

"Not mad. Disappointed, maybe." Verity crossed her arms. "What do you say, kids? Shall we make our guest tell us his best and worst moments of the week?"

Keenan's head snapped up, mischief stamped on his features. "Yeah, Mr. Sawtelle, tell us. Where do I rank in the worst moments of the week?" He crossed his arms and lounged back against his chair.

Verity tensed, but Garrett laughed. "Finding a new kid on my list is always one of the low points, but getting to know your family was one of my high points."

"Only one? Not the very highest?" Verity clapped her hand over her mouth. "I can't believe I just said that."

Garrett's lips parted in a slow grin. "My best point of the week was the game on Wednesday night."

Verity didn't understand.

"When I saw the next outfielder for the Maple Notch Patriots at work."

Garrett wasn't talking about Verity anymore.

"What do you say, Keenan? Are you interested in playing ball for your school?"

Garrett kept his tone light, but he focused his eyes on Keenan. Interest sparked in the boy's face, before his I-don't-care mask dropped back into place. He lifted a shoulder in a careless shrug. "Maybe."

Before Garrett took the next step, he looked at Verity. Her eyes had gone blank, her mind on some other track. He should have asked her first, but the idea had seemed so right.

She blinked. "That will give you a lot to keep up with. You've got school, and your hours at the museum, and church." She snapped her fingers. "But none of that sounds like much fun, does it? As long as you can keep up with school, I'm game."

"That's good." Garrett reached into the briefcase resting against his chair leg and pulled out the parent permission form. "I brought the info sheet. Aside from the doctor's form, all you need to do is to show up at practice next spring."

Keenan practically grabbed the paper from Garrett's hand. "Don't I have to try out or something?"

Garrett shook his head. "Everyone who meets the academic qualifications—no grade below a C, that's a piece of cake, right?—and who attends all the practices has a spot on the team, and the coach makes sure everyone plays a couple of minutes in each game." He winked at Verity. "But as good as you are, I bet you might be a starter."

A smile skipped across Keenan's face before it turned into a scowl.

"You're lucky that you're tall," Garrett said. "I always had to work extra hard, because I'm just average-sized."

Verity looked him over head to toe, long enough for him to squirm. She turned away, as if embarrassed. "Curtis— Keenan's father—was tall."

"You must look like your father, kid. You've got your mother's eyes, but…" Garrett decided he was getting into uncertain territory, where no truant officer deserved to go.

Des left the table and came back with a picture frame. "This is my dad."

The glass had lots of thumbprints from frequent handling. Curtis Clark had his arm draped over his daughter's shoulders, and she looked up at him with adoration in her eyes. In his army fatigues, he looked like he could have been a model for a recruitment poster. "He looks like a good man." Garrett handed the frame back to Des. "How old were you when your father died?"

"I was the same age Mason is now." Des hugged the picture to her chest before she darted to her bedroom to drop off the photo.

Garrett looked at Verity. "Touchy subject?"

Verity waved her hands in an uncertain gesture. "She's been missing him more lately." She opened her mouth to say more, but the girl returned to her seat and her mother stopped speaking.

"My favorite thing this week." Des stood a book in front of her. "Remembering the fishing trip with Dad. I wish it was springtime, so I could go fishing again."

Garrett almost offered to take her, but stopped himself in time. Des didn't miss fishing as much as she missed her dad. Another man would only make it worse. He turned to a different topic. "Hey, are either one of you thinking about spending a weekend at the cave this year?"

Their common ancestor, Sally Reid, had lived in a cave during the Revolutionary War, while her family worked their farm in secret from the Tories. A weekend at the cave had turned into a rite of passage for her descendants. Amity Finch coordinated the adventures, and invited all descendants to come for a weekend at different times throughout the year. "Your mother and I both went to the cave the same summer."

Verity nodded. "Amity wants to build it into a week-long life-in-colonial-times event. She's even talking about getting an archaeologist to dig for the original cabin from the 1760s."

Keenan poured himself a cup of coffee. Garrett watched Verity watch her son, but she didn't comment. When Keenan sat down, he took two pancakes. "Aunt Amity is bugging me, telling me I gotta go this year."

"Do you get to go hunting and fishing and stuff?" Mason's eyes grew big.

"I guess so. Finding our way through the woods."

"What woods?" Des asked.

"There were woods along both sides of the river back then. They've chopped most of them down but there are still a few," Verity said.

"Can I go too?" Mason practically jumped up and down in his chair.

"Not yet, squirt. You have to be at least eleven." Keenan shadowboxed his brother.

"I'm brave enough." Mason puffed out his chest, then blew it out. "Why do I always have to be too young for anything fun?"

"Think of it this way. You're still small enough to play

in McDonald's Playland." Keenan grinned at him. "I was too tall when I was four. That made me mad, too."

"Your turn," Garrett said as Verity dished another portion of the omelet on his plate and refilled his coffee cup. "You haven't told us your best moment of the week." He already could guess her worst moment, and he wouldn't ask.

She paused long enough to make sure she didn't overpour her coffee cup. The urn was empty, so she turned off the burner. She took a deep sip and sighed.

"Morning coffee is one of my favorite things. 'Simply remember my favorite things…'" she sang happily. "I got a nice comment on my blog. This lady's son just started chemotherapy, and she said my posts encourage her to keep going. If God can use everything we went through to help someone else, that's a good thing, isn't it?"

Mason nodded so hard that Garrett could have sworn his head would fly off. "When I was in the hospital, I wanted to be brave so the girl in the room at the end of the hall wouldn't be so scared."

"That's good. Do you still get to see her now?"

Mason hesitated only a moment. "No. She went to heaven, to be with Jesus. I asked God to send my dad to Junie, because she might be scared."

Verity wasn't the only one with tears in her eyes.

Garrett enjoyed the banter. He had never visited a truant with such strong family ties before. For all of his illnesses, Mason seemed like a typical eight-year-old, if a little on the small side. The older kids, well, they had stress, but what child their age didn't? Garrett's confidence meter jumped over the top after the breakfast they shared, and he didn't really want to leave.

At nine-thirty, Mason dashed into the living room and turned on cartoons.

"Aunt Amity asked me to come in this morning," Keenan said. The doorbell rang. "There she is."

"I'll pick you up this afternoon." Verity turned to Garrett. "Do you need to speak with him some more?"

Garrett shook his head.

Des rinsed the dishes before arranging them in the dishwasher.

Verity lingered over her coffee, not speaking. After draining it, she said, "Aren't you supposed to interview me or something?"

Garrett's good feelings stretched thin. This was a business visit, after all.

Chapter 5

The light dimmed in Garrett's face. Verity would do almost anything to make him feel better, for the excitement that lightened his features to reappear. He should be a teacher or a coach, not a truant officer. *Shame on you, Verity. Thinking his job is beneath him.* It demanded a lot from those who cared, like Garrett.

"You could call it an in-home visit." His rich bass conveyed a brisk, no-nonsense attitude. He could be either a big brother or a drill sergeant, whichever was needed.

"So what are your findings? Did we pass the test?" Foolish question. If Keenan hadn't skipped school, Garrett wouldn't be here.

Garrett tapped his fingers on the table. "Actually, I'm impressed. My mom stopped fixing us Saturday morning breakfast by the time I was Mason's age. She kept fixing us Sunday morning coffee cake for a few more years." His smile whispered across his mouth at the memory. "I'd like the see the rest of the apartment."

Verity thought about the pile of clothes stacked by the washing machine, the stripped beds in the boys' room, Des's books and papers scattered across the desk in their room. She'd only had time to pick up the living room, but saying no would be worse than showing him the mess. "Bedrooms are back this way."

In the hall, he looked at the family pictures hanging on the wall, including the last picture of the five of them, when Mason was a year old. "I should get another family portrait made. Now that Mason is doing so well…" She swallowed. "Last year, I put off getting pictures."

"You wanted the real Mason and not a picture on the wall." Garrett nodded. "The snaps I saw in the living room told me something else about you."

"What's that?"

"Your absence in the family photos. You're the photographer." He shrugged. "Most mothers are."

Verity giggled. Her jeans caught on an open drawer, and she stumbled. Garrett reached out a hand to steady her. As soon as she righted herself, he let go. Glaring at the offending drawer, she threw a dirty shirt in the laundry basket and closed the drawer.

Before she could pick up the basket, Garrett's long arms already had it in his grasp. "Where do you want this?"

"The washing machine is straight ahead, next to the bathroom." He couldn't miss it. Clothes stacked on clothes waiting a washing.

"Saturday is laundry day, I take it." Garrett set the basket on top of the dryer. "It is for me most weeks, as well." He put his hand on the bathroom door. "Mind if I use it?"

Verity shook her head. She busied herself loading the washer.

The wash cycle had just started when Garrett stepped out of the bathroom. "Who sleeps in this bedroom?" He knocked on the door and entered when no one answered. "Des's?" He held up a pink princess notebook and a copy of the latest teen book phenomenon.

"Yes. Hers and mine. We share." Verity felt a little ashamed that she shared a room with her daughter, and for letting her read "trash," as her mother might have called it.

Garrett frowned at that announcement. "It's better if you can have separate rooms."

Tension seized Verity's throat, and she made herself breathe. "I know that. But do you know the difference in cost between a two-bedroom, one-bath apartment, and a three-bedroom, two-bath rental?"

Garrett flashed her a grin. "It's okay." He opened the closets—one, organized by color, to make it easy to match-and-go. Des's probably wasn't worse than teenage girls everywhere, but Verity was thankful she didn't have to share the space with her daughter. After a cursory glance, he shut the doors and brought his hands together. "It's unfortunate that you and Des have to share a room. When you can, look into getting that three-bedroom apartment." He stopped, his face turning serious. "If social services ever gets involved, they might make an issue of it."

Garrett hated what his questions did to Verity, the way he intruded on her privacy. Some mothers would be hiding drugs from police. They didn't flinch when a truant officer arrived. But Verity Clark wasn't most mothers.

"If that happens, a couple of the places on the resource list I gave you can help you find something. You might want to apply for help with housing now. It can take a long time to get approval."

"Assistance?" Verity backed down as if she had never heard the word before. "I can't do that. My family…" She hung her head, ashamed at her predicament.

Too bad Verity hadn't inherited the Bailey mansion instead of her sister. The news made a splash at the time, but Felicity had surprised the town by opening a bed-and-breakfast and transforming the aging building into an amazing example of historical restoration.

"When I left town with Curtis, I never thought I'd come back for anything more than occasional visits. We hadn't decided where we wanted to retire before he died."

"Final expenses can eat up a bunch of money, I know that." Garrett had run into the "Assistance? Not me" attitude before. "The purpose of housing assistance is to help people like you. You've run into a spot of difficulty. You were handling things okay until Mason got sick last year."

Nodding, she deflated as she blew out her breath. "I suppose you want to see the boys' bedroom next."

"Ayuh." Garrett took stock of the room as he turned and surveyed the four walls. This room was smaller than the girls' master bedroom. Keenan slept on the top bunk, so he didn't have a handy hiding place beneath his bed.

Garrett ran his hands beneath the mattress, trying not to anticipate what he would find. A Bible—that should please Verity, a pack of gum. Double points for none of the magazines teenage boys salivated over, a stash of cigarettes or something worse.

"Does Keenan have a girlfriend?" A good-looking kid like Keenan should attract a girl's attention. Mom might not know about it, though.

Verity's eyes glazed over as she considered the question. "Not that I know of."

Toy cars shared floor space with a basketball. A sheet in a khaki print was draped over the computer.

"Is it okay for the boys to room together?" Verity picked up a pair of jeans, sniffed them before ducking out of the room to toss them into the washer.

"Yes."

"Keenan would like to have a room of his own. And none of the kids can invite friends to spend the night. We don't have space for guests."

The washing machine stopped. "Do you mind?"

Shaking his head no, Garrett continued his perusal of the room. The more he learned of Keenan, the less likely it seemed that he would skip school just because. Until they learned "why," he might skip again if provoked. Garrett knocked against the wood of the bunk as he climbed down.

Des stood in the doorway. She looked around the room. "They don't let me come in here."

"I guess it's a guy thing." Garrett looked at the girl thoughtfully. She was in the best position to know where her brother went instead of school. The middle school was separated from the high school by a covered hallway. But if she hadn't told her mother after all this time, Garrett doubted she would tell him.

"Cars and comic books." Des nodded her head. "I don't let them into my room, either."

Nodding, Garrett poked into a few bags and came up empty. "I'm done in here."

Des stepped aside and Garrett left the room.

Verity dropped assorted socks and shirts in the washing machine and started it going. The dryer rumbled in the background. "Can I help you with something else?"

Before Garrett could answer, Mason ran down the hall. "Kow-pow! Lightning strike." He sang a ditty from a popular cartoon. "Mom, I want to wear my lightning shirt today."

She shook her head. "Sorry, squirt. It's in the laundry."

Mason ignored her, picking through the clothes. Verity inserted herself in front of her son and pointed toward the living room. "Go."

Mason looked at Garrett. "I guess." He shut the door behind him.

Des reappeared, her hair carefully styled in a casual mess. "If you don't watch out, he'll burst out of the door, pretending he's a superhero, and run you over."

"We'd better move," Verity said. "Unless there's something more you want to see?"

Garrett shook his head, and they walked toward the living room.

When he sat on the couch, Des sat next to him. "Do you have any children, Mr. Sawtelle?"

Garrett shook his head. "Not yet. I'm not married."

"Kow-pow!" Mason burst from his room, a pair of nun-chucks in his hands. "Mighty Mason saves the day." He twirled the play weapon in his hands. "I got you now."

Verity closed her eyes, obviously tired.

"Hey, fella, you want to play catch with me outside? You, too, Des, if you want."

Verity's eyes, seas of aquamarine, flew open. "You don't have to do that. You must have other plans for your weekend."

"Who can resist a game of catch?" Garrett dug for his keys.

Mason reappeared, a baseball mitt on his hand.

"Do I have your permission to take them to the park?"

Verity moved to the windows. Sunlight streamed in, bathing the floor in dancing dust mites. "There won't be too many more pretty days like this before winter sets in. Let's all go."

"Mom's coming?" Mason jumped up and down. He opened the front door.

"Get your jacket."

Des dashed into her room, reappearing in a hooded sweatshirt with the Patriots logo against a deep green background. She put a matching ball cap on her head. A worn leather glove covered her left hand, a wooden bat tucked under her arm and a ball in her right hand. "Catch, Mr. Sawtelle."

"Don't..." Verity said.

The ball reached Garrett's hands before Verity finished her protest. "That was a good throw." Garrett handed the ball back to Des as they left the house.

"I played Little League every year, until Mason got sick." Des scowled at her mother. "None of us got to do anything much while he was sick."

Verity's shoulders drooped, but she responded brightly. "I'm sorry about that. But you can play this spring. The softball league and at school, if you want to."

"I hope so." Des didn't sound too willing to let her mother off the hook for the missing spring season.

"I want to play soccer," Mason said. He dropped the softball and it hopped its way down the stairs outside the apartment.

A curtain twitched in the apartment below Verity's when they piled into the cars. Raising children with only a floor separating her from another family must be difficult. "Do your neighbors ever complain?"

The guilt on Verity's face gave him her answer before she said a word.

Verity headed for her car, and Garrett called to her. "You can ride with me."

She didn't even pause, unlocking the door. "I have to pick up Keenan before long. We can go our separate ways if I take my car."

The lady had to keep a dozen balls in the air at the same time.

Mason had already climbed into Garrett's car. "Climb in, if you like."

Des squeezed in beside Mason. The three of them reminded him of times Mom and Dad came to watch his games when he was a boy.

Verity had promised herself that she would stay at the park for an hour. If the kids didn't want to leave by then, she would shop and pick up Keenan at the end of his shift. Instead, every time Mason hit the ball, she cheered him on. Whenever Des caught one, Verity jumped to her feet. She couldn't tear herself away.

Garrett looked as natural on the diamond as he had on a football field, not the kind of man who belonged in an office. At last, Garrett called the play to a halt. "Hey, is Keenan free to talk with me when he finishes at the museum?"

"He is." Verity called to pass on the message. "Mr. Sawtelle will pick you up after work."

Keenan grunted. "Okay, I guess."

Verity turned to Garrett. "He's expecting you."

"Good." Garrett scratched a spot on his head behind his ear. "We have a great youth Sunday school at church. You might want to check it out sometime."

When he mentioned church, Des's head jerked up.

"Youth includes everyone in middle school and high school. Sometimes the class meets together, other times they split up."

Verity shook her head. "I don't know. We attend the Community Church, downtown."

"Can't we visit? Please?" Mason whined.

She'd always had a hard time saying no to her youngest son. "When are your services?"

"Classes start at nine. I'll be by at 8:45 to pick you up. In a car, with seats for all." Before she could change her mind, he had pulled away.

What had she just agreed to? They headed home.

"Mom, can we have pizza?" Mason pointed to his favorite pizza place as they drove by. "It's been the best day."

"Not today." Hardly ever. Verity preferred to spend any extra money on more important things.

Mason shrugged. "Garrett says I hit the ball really good." Sometime over the morning their guest had moved from "Mr. Sawtelle" to the informal "Garrett."

"He threw the ball where you could hit it really easy," Des said.

"Did not," Mason said.

Verity held her breath, ready to intercede if the argument escalated, but Des settled into her corner.

"You did a good job catching those balls." Verity tilted her rearview mirror so Des could see her face. "I am sorry about last year. This year will be different, I promise."

"As long as Keenan doesn't get into trouble or Mason stays healthy. Or Aunt Felicity doesn't need your help over at the tea shop." Des held her ball glove above her face, blocking the rearview mirror both ways.

Another boatload of guilt washed over Verity. *I have confessed my sins. I am forgiven.* Another voice answered, *Yeah, but you still have to deal with the consequences of your bad decisions.* Every day, she let her kids down in some important way, and they kept slipping farther and farther away.

As soon as they got home, Mason turned on the TV, and Des activated the computer to play games online. Verity pulled clothes from the dryer.

"Mom." Mason trotted down the hall. "Garrett said he used to play soccer in the fall and in the spring. He says it's too late for the fall, but can I play in the spring? Please?"

"Well…" Verity's mind went wild imagining dangers

for a cancer survivor, although the risks were minimal. "We'll have to ask your doctor."

Mason continued as if he hadn't heard. "I bet it'll be fun. He says their Sunday school teacher isn't an old lady with white hair and big glasses."

"Mrs. K. is a great teacher." Des was looking out the window, not seeming to listen to the conversation until she spoke.

"I bet Garrett is a great teacher. I wish he taught my class but he said he doesn't."

"Can you please stop talking about Mr. Sawtelle in every sentence?" Twisting around, Des glared at her brother.

"He said I could call him Garrett, since we're family. Didn't he, Mom?"

"You're too much." Des returned to her window watching.

"When we're with other people, it's probably best to call him Mr. Sawtelle." Verity intervened before their argument escalated.

"Maybe I can call him Uncle Garrett. I don't have any uncles."

"Uncle Travis." Des sounded proud to prove him wrong.

"Oh, yeah." Mason frowned. "And Garrett said I couldn't call him uncle, either."

The anger in Des's eyes scared Verity a bit, but her daughter shrugged and reached for a pair of earbuds. "I need some peace and quiet."

Mason kept chatting about Garrett, poking Des to make her listen. Whenever he did, Des sang the song she was listening to, singing louder and more off-key with each poke.

Verity felt like she had driven a hundred miles by bedtime. Garrett had hit a home run with Mason, but Des seemed ambivalent.

Her request to join Garrett and Mason in the park had surprised Verity, but maybe she just wanted a chance to play ball. Garrett encouraged Mason the way he would any young player, but he had solid words of praise for Des. "She's good, Verity. Seriously good. She deserves to play." His words weighed on Verity's conscience.

But after their return, Des wouldn't say a single word about the afternoon. Verity had been there, knew nothing bad had happened. Perhaps her daughter felt guilty for playing with a man other than her dad. Maybe even unhappy that her mother came, making it feel like a family—except they weren't a family.

Putting a note about church on her calendar, she almost called Garrett to cancel the visit.

But she didn't. The good points made it worth the risk. At the park, he had reminded her of what having a man in the family felt like. She wanted that again, for her children, but mostly for herself.

Chapter 6

Garrett pulled in front of the museum as Keenan came out. He was talking with his aunt while she locked the door. Even in twenty-first-century clothing, her simple style made her look like she could belong to a past era. The three Finch sisters were as pretty as a field of wildflowers, each one unique.

No one would ever mistake Keenan for anything but a millennium baby, more animated today than Garrett had ever seen him. Maybe the job had jostled a latent interest in history that his teacher hadn't reached. After all, the blood of people who shaped Maple Notch's history ran in his veins.

A current of compliance under protest sizzled beneath the service. Given the right incentive, he'd bolt again.

Keenan looked up and down the street, as if looking for his mother's car. When he checked his watch, Garrett stuck his head out the window and waved.

Keenan came to the car and motioned for Garrett to

lower the window. "Mom said you were coming. What do you want with me?"

Borderline rude—Garrett had dealt with worse. "It's getting late in the season, but I always enjoy a hike at Camel's Hump State Park. We can walk for an hour or so, chat in privacy and stop by a burger joint on the way home."

Keenan shrugged. "Okay."

"Unless you want us to get a bite now, talk over food and go home in time to do homework while you're watching college football on TV?"

"Hockey," Keenan said. "I like to watch hockey."

Garrett considered that. "I'm on a curling team. You know, the Olympic sport where you push the stone down the ice with a broom?"

"They play that around here?" Keenan said.

"It's getting more popular all the time." When Keenan sneered at that remark, Garrett said, "Hey, it's harder than it looks. The skating complex they built at the old Nash Ice Rink sponsors a couple of teams, one for adults and one for kids. We have a couple of players who are trying out for the Olympic team." He kept an eye on the boy, seeing if he found a hint of interest. If there was, Garrett couldn't find it.

"You like basketball and hockey. You're having fun with the museum, and I saw the books in your room. I can give you a list of books I like that don't show up on most reading lists, if you're interested."

Keenan blew out a breath long enough to blow out all the candles on his grandfather's birthday cake. "You don't have to play big brother with me. My dad died defending his country. End of story. Yeah, it was tough, but I'm okay now."

"Your mother…"

"Why are you hanging around Mom? If there's anything that needs doing, I'll do it for her."

Keenan bristled with wounded adolescent pride, but Garrett had waded through those waters before. "I figured you would feel more comfortable talking with me away from my office."

"We did that this morning." Keenan shifted his angle, so Garrett got the full-on glare. "So why now?"

"This morning, I was talking with your mother. Kids don't tell their parents everything."

"And you think I will talk to you instead? Excuse my language, but that's delusional."

Definitely a Finch talking. A lot of boys would use a word of the four-letter variety instead.

"Maybe, maybe not. But I hope you will learn to trust me. I want the best for you. And for better or for worse, that means finishing school. Even if your sole goal in life is to clean buildings, you need a diploma."

"I don't want to sweep floors for a living." Keenan sounded insulted that Garrett had suggested it.

They reached the entrance to the park, and Garrett found a parking place. "It's your time to decide. Do you want to hike, or do you want to go for burgers and head home?"

Keenan stared out the window, looking at a hummingbird hovering at a bird feeder, wings beating so fast that one could barely see the body with the naked eye. But he didn't blink once. Finally he turned back to Garrett. "I'll go on the hike." He opened the door, drawing his ball cap over his eyes and zipping up his hoodie.

Garrett opened the trunk and dug out his backpack, slipping his arms through. It held water and trail mix, and a journal if he felt in the mood. He added his phone, which doubled as a camera, and his wallet, along with a sweater, and joined Keenan at the guard shack. They stopped by the trail map board to find the best route.

"Here's the short trail, if you want to get home soon." At three-quarters of a mile loop, almost every visitor could manage it.

"For old grandmas who need to rest on those benches. No, thank you." Keenan's hand hovered over the board. Garrett guessed that he liked the looks of the advanced trail, as it promised a view from the top of Mount Ellen.

Garrett had to disappoint him. "The Mount Ellen trail is closed for the winter season. They never know when a snowstorm will pass over and cut hikers off from rescue."

Keenan scowled. "How about this one?" He pointed to a three-mile loop. "The map says there's a diner along the path."

A three-mile hike would take an hour, longer if they stopped to eat. Keenan's choice surprised Garrett, in the best of ways. "Let's do it."

The boy jogged in place, the hood of his jacket gathered around his face like an athlete in training. "Ready to run?"

No easy stroll, and that's the way Garrett liked it. "Anytime."

Laughing, Keenan took off and Garrett followed behind. The kid probably thought he had the old man beat. Let him find out for himself.

Four hours—Verity set an alarm. That's how long it had taken her to pick up, sort, wash, dry and put away the laundry they had collected over the week. She kept thinking she'd do it faster the next time, but she never did. Paid laundry machines saved time, but she had chosen this apartment because it came with the appliances to save money. Money versus time, the constant battle.

Des dived into the closet as soon as Verity put everything away and held one of her mother's sweaters against her.

Verity could read the longing in her eyes. "Go ahead. Try it on."

"May I?" Des didn't wait for a second yes before she pulled it over her head. The pale yellow cashmere was one of Verity's favorites, but it looked even better on Des than it did on her. Her little girl was growing up.

Des looked in the mirror, frowned and returned to the closet. Bending down, she checked out the shoes in their boxes, and removed a pair of gold strapped sandals, the highest heels that Verity owned. When her mother didn't protest, she buckled them on and strutted around awkwardly in the shoes. With each step, her long legs became steadier. Glowing, she struck a pose, a girl on the verge of womanhood. Satisfied, she removed the sweater and hung it on the hanger.

Des slouched on the bed, studying the polish on her toenails.

"You want me to paint them for you?" Verity studied the choices on top of her dresser. "I have Ruby Red, Vivid Violet and Perfect Peach." She twisted the cap of the Ruby Red, Des's usual choice.

Des wiggled her toes before folding her legs under the bed. "Not today. No matter what I put on, I'm an ugly duckling."

"Oh, honey." Verity sat next to her daughter. "Look at the mirror." She tilted Des's face, making her look.

"Ugly duckling. Like I said." She twisted back the walnut-brown strands that kept falling in her face.

Verity could argue about the beauty hidden underneath Des's awkward adolescence. But her daughter's angst had little to do with facts. "I could remind you that the story ends with the ugly duckling turning into a beautiful swan—like you will be someday."

Des scoffed.

"Are you feeling like the odd one out?"

Des scrunched her face. "Yeah. I guess. Mason was so sick. And now Keenan's giving you grief. And you're so busy with Garrett, you don't have time for me anymore."

While Verity thought how best to answer, Des spoke again. "I wish Dad was still here. Nothing's been good since he died."

Guilt slammed into Verity. Tears tumbled down her cheeks, and she didn't hold them back. She pulled Des into her arms. "I'm sorry, honey. I miss your dad, too."

The sobs stopped but neither one of them let go. Verity was ready to invite Des to cook dinner with her when the front door opened.

"I'm home." Keenan's voice boomed across the empty living room and down the hall.

"Mind if I come in?" Garrett added.

"Yes." Des broke away from Verity's shoulder and jumped up from the bed. "Go ahead, Mom. I know you want to see him." She climbed onto the top bunk, wiping away the good feeling of the afternoon.

Des needed her, but Garrett was waiting in the living room. Wishing their bedroom had a half bath, Verity wiped away the tears with facial tissue and dabbed a bit of face cream on her cheeks. Drawing in a deep breath, she left the room.

"Did I come at a bad time?" Garrett stood at the door, looking uncertain.

"Nothing im—er, urgent." Verity winced at her slip. Of course her conversation with Des was important.

Garrett kept his jacket on, as if he intended to leave soon. He leaned in close and spoke quietly. "Keenan and I had a good visit. Ask him to tell you about the buck he scared away in the woods." He scanned his phone to a photo of a five-point buck looking straight at the camera, with Keenan's face in profile.

Tears jumped into Verity's eyes. Keenan looked so handsome, so grown-up.

"If you like it, I can send it to your email."

"Yes, please." She'd load it as the backdrop to her computer. But what about Des? She'd have to get photos of each child.

Her phone buzzed, and she found Garrett had already forwarded the picture. "That was quick. Thanks."

His phone clicked, and she realized Garrett had taken her picture. Out of the corner of her eye, she saw her daughter hanging out by the bedroom door. "Des and I were about to make my famous chili."

"Chili?" Garrett raised an eyebrow. "That's an unusual dinner in Maple Notch."

"But not in Killeen, where we lived after our honeymoon. Curtis used to call it our honeymoon specialty. We ate it on our anniversary every year, but…"

Des had walked a few steps down the hallway. "We eat it now to remember Dad." She said it like a challenge.

Garrett reached up and scratched behind his ear. "That's a good tradition. We still eat my grandma's green bean casserole every Thanksgiving."

"You and half the country." But Verity smiled. "Thank you for spending time with Keenan this afternoon." She couldn't ask about it, not with all of her children listening in.

"Are you eating supper with us, Garrett?" Mason ran out of the bathroom in his cartoon pajamas.

Garrett glanced over Verity's shoulder, where Des had made it to the archway into the kitchen. "Maybe we can make plans for dinner on Sunday. I still plan on picking you up in the morning."

* * *

Sunday morning, Garrett couldn't stop pacing. Repeating the week's memory verse, from the parable about the prodigal son, left him unsettled. All the children he had tried to help paraded through his mind. With each step, he remembered another case. He prayed that at least one out of a hundred of his lost sheep became productive members of society. Keenan was close to number one hundred.

With that, he circled back to his anticipation of seeing Verity this morning. The clock showed it was time to leave for church, and he headed out the door.

He had grown up in the Community Church, and come to know the Lord there. But when he returned from college, he wanted something different.

Garrett hoped, prayed, that the Clarks would enjoy his church. The name—Bumblebee Christian Fellowship—made people smile, but it was located on the west bank of the Bumblebee River, which split Maple Notch in half. Someday he would like to walk with Verity along the river, on a path extending from the Nash ice arena to the Reid Cave.

However, Garrett had no business asking her for a walk, or anything else. Once again, he reminded himself to keep their relationship on a professional level. Friendship was good, but dating? No way.

The church was only a few miles away, another advantage for Garrett. The Clarks were ready when he arrived. After he let them off at the front, he parked in a far corner, leaving space for latecomers and visitors.

When he sprinted across the parking lot, he saw Anne Reid—one of the church's official greeters—speaking with them. Given what he knew of Anne, she had already learned Verity's life history before he made it inside the church.

As soon as he entered, Anne brought Keenan and Des to his side. "Mrs. Clark tells me that you invited her to worship with us. Keenan, Des, do you know that Mr. Sawtelle is one of your Sunday school teachers?"

Keenan looked at the ground. "He didn't tell me, but Aaron did."

"Aaron?" Anne beamed. "He's my grandson. How good to have a friend here already. He came with me this morning."

They walked down the hall together until they reached Mason's classroom. Verity looked at Garrett, as if wishing she could go with him. Garrett hesitated a moment too long. Keenan and Des had gone ahead.

"Don't worry about us, Mom." Des looked back from the top of the stairs. "Our class is down here. See you later."

While teaching, God cleared Garrett's mind of personal matters, as He often did. Everyone in the group knew his job, and a few of them had been his clients. He shared how he was happy when a client did well, and how much greater was the rejoicing in heaven. He introduced the two Clarks without explaining how they had met.

After the lesson, the kids split into two groups. Garrett peeked through the windows in the doors. Keenan and Aaron had hit it off, which gave him hope. Des, on the other hand, sat apart from the other girls, empty chairs on either side of her.

When the teacher introduced Des to the others, one of the other girls, Hayley, moved to the chair next to Des. *Way to go, Hayley.*

After checking on both classes, Garrett headed down the hall. Mason was smaller than the other children his age, but no one meeting him for the first time would guess at his bout with cancer.

As he climbed the stairs, the door to the young-adult classroom opened and Verity was the first out. She looked puzzled.

"Did you enjoy class?" Garrett asked.

"Very much." Verity looked toward the staircase. "Excuse me, but I want to be there when Mason's class dismisses."

Garrett took one step to follow her, but instead he approached the head deacon. "Can I make an announcement today? I want to remind everyone to sign up for the ice skating party on Saturday, although last-minute guests are allowed."

"Sure."

Verity had arrived at the door to the sanctuary, where Keenan was talking to her. She nodded and smiled, and Keenan walked away from her, going front and center of the platform, where the other teens sat.

If Garrett had his way, Keenan and Des would both be at the ice skating party. Even more, he wanted Verity to be there, too. She deserved to smile, and he wanted to be the one to make it happen.

Chapter 7

"Go ahead and sit with the others, if you want," Verity told Des. In the pews in front of the pulpit, Keenan sat in the middle of a group of boys, laughing. Girls entered through a side door and joined them.

Des shook her head, looking uncomfortable. Instead of hugging her, Verity asked, "Where would you like to sit?"

"Up there." Des pointed to the side close to the praise band, while Mason ran ahead. Several people Verity knew welcomed them. After setting aside her disappointment that Garrett hadn't joined them, Verity settled with her family on the third row.

With guitars, drums and keyboards, the music was not what she was used to in her more traditional church. By the time the sermon started, the vigorous style of worship had worn Verity on one hand and energized her on the other.

Before she knew it, the sermon had ended and announcements were being made as the ushers took the offering. The money she had set aside for her tithe burned a hole in her purse. Give it here, where she had worshipped, or send it to the church where her membership implied her support? Torn, she put half into the offering plate as it passed.

With the question settled in her mind, she listened as Garrett announced a skating party for the youth on Saturday. Des perked up. She loved to skate, and didn't get to go often enough. "Can I, Mom?" she whispered. Verity nodded.

What about Keenan? Could he go, given his duties at the museum and keeping his grades up? When he was grounded? This was a church activity. Helping a teen take responsibility for himself was easy to say, but hard to figure out when the child ran into trouble.

When the service ended, they were surrounded by well-wishers. Mason slipped away in search of promised doughnuts.

Keenan found them by the entrance. "I signed up for the skating party. Is that okay?"

What was that saying, better to ask forgiveness than permission? "You may go——if you keep up with your schoolwork and job at the museum."

"Mom."

Verity suspected Keenan's glare was for the sake of the kids around him.

"Ayuh. Those are my rules. Oh, and Des is going, too."

While they added Des's name to the list, Garrett headed in her direction, with a woman at his side who looked familiar. Who was she—Jerri, no, Ginny Sawtelle. Garrett's sister.

"Hi, Verity. I'm Ginny Roberts, Garrett's..."

"Sister." They shook hands. "It's been a while." That

was an understatement. She hadn't seen Ginny since Curtis's funeral.

"Garrett suggested we talk. I got divorced a few years ago, and joined the group we have here for single parents. My kids are grown now, but I still like to attend. You don't have to be a church member or anything." Ginny gave her the details, about child care and the Tuesday night meeting. She handed Verity a worship bulletin, with the time scheduled. "I wrote my phone number down in case you want to call."

"I'll think about it," Verity said.

A girl close to Des's age pulled Ginny away, leaving Garrett alone with Verity. He put his hands in his pockets. "So, what did you think of Bumblebee Fellowship?

"Different."

"In a good way, I hope." Garrett grinned. "I'm glad the kids are skating with us. Does Mason like to skate?"

Verity stiffened and forced herself to relax. It was time to let Mason act like a normal eight-year-old. "I don't know."

Mason rejoined her, telltale sugar outlining his mouth. "Can I go skating with Keenan and Des?" He bounced up and down on his heels.

"Honey, it's for the big kids. We'll do something special together on Saturday instead, okay?"

Mason brightened. "Can we get ice cream?"

Ice cream in the middle of winter. "Why not?"

"They have family skates on Saturday mornings. Lower rates for a family package. In case you're interested some other time." Garrett hesitated. "I suppose that means you won't be there on Saturday?"

"Just long enough to drop them off."

On Monday morning, Verity thought about Garrett's

question while she attempted to scan the newspaper and computer websites for jobs.

Garrett wanted them to skate together. Did he want to see her again—or was he warning her to spend more time with her family?

She didn't know. It shouldn't matter, but it did. Dating fell far down on her list of priorities.

She read through the help-wanted ads again. Mostly she found jobs for seasonal workers. And of the jobs listed, none of the hours matched Mason's school schedule. What about Felicity's tea shop? With Mason doing better, she could work without the fear of unexpected absences.

Barring any more problems with Keenan.

Verity picked up her phone, hit the speed-dial number, then turned it off before it could ring. Tilting back in her chair, she looked at the ceiling. "God, will You give me a sign if I should help at the tea shop?"

The phone in her hand rang—Felicity. Verity smiled as she hit the talk button. "Hello, sis."

"Hi. How did you like the new church?"

Verity told her about the classes, the friends that Keenan had made, the upcoming ice skating party, the single-parents group tomorrow night.

"So you liked it. I'm glad." Felicity launched right into the reason for her call. "I have a problem this week. My chef's parents flew in for a surprise visit and he asked if he could take some time off. I don't want you back permanently, but I thought I would ask you first, before I look elsewhere."

Verity laughed. "I was thinking about asking you if you needed any help during the holidays. I bet you're overloaded with orders for muffins for Christmas parties."

Felicity confirmed her suspicions, and together they identified other days she needed help. Her head waitress had scheduled a few vacation days, Felicity had a couple of large cookie, cupcake and muffin orders to fill and the B and B would be full for every day of the school vacation.

"I'll be there in the morning." Verity took hope from this small sign.

Garrett walked into his office, whistling, on Monday morning. The Christmas bells his assistant hung from the doorknob jingled. A Douglas fir tree stood in the corner, decorated with every school-and-winter-themed ornament Marcia could find.

"You sound happy this morning." Marcia handed Garrett a note. "Mrs. Clark called. She said she would call back later."

Mrs. Clark. Underlined twice and in bold print. His heart raced, and he knew that Marcia's keen eyes read his reaction even if he tried to hide it. Why had Verity called so early on a Monday morning?

He hung his coat on the rack, walked into his office and closed the door. Two weeks of winter vacation lay ahead. It could work to Keenan's advantage, giving him the break he needed so he could head back to school with a fresh mind and a clean slate.

But what if the break in routine undid the progress he had made? Perhaps Verity wanted to discuss the situation when the boy wasn't around, before the office closed. She didn't answer her personal phone, so he tried the phone number Marcia had written on the note.

"Felici'Tea's Shoppe." The treble of Verity's voice sounded as cheerful as Christmas bells to his ear.

"Hi, Verity, it's me." Stupid. "Garrett. I heard you called."

"Oh, yes, Garrett. I want to talk with you, but I'm caught up in things right now. Can we talk after lunch?"

Garrett agreed. When the noon hour approached, he drove to the tea shop for lunch. The server greeted him and started toward a table by the front door. "I'd rather have a table near the kitchen, if that's okay."

Tanya smiled as if she knew the reason for his request. "Verity and Felicity are working on a large Christmas cupcake order, but I'll let them know you are here."

Garrett lingered over his lunch—an open-faced turkey sandwich on homemade bread with a side salad with cranberry vinaigrette—but neither baker exited the kitchen while he waited. Possible reasons for her call raced around his mind. Probably about Keenan and nothing personal. He drank a final cup of coffee, received change for his bill and stood to leave when Verity came out. Flour dusted her apron, a few dark wisps escaped her hairnet. "Garrett. I was going to call when we were done."

"I was hungry." He patted the table while he signaled for another cup of coffee. "Will you be available anytime soon?"

She glanced back through the door. "I promised to help Felicity finish the order. Half an hour, maybe?"

Garrett nodded, although he felt a little disappointed. One of his clients had left a message about an upcoming date in juvenile court. He noted the court date on his calendar—three days before Christmas, in the middle of what was supposed to be a two-week winter break. Tired of waiting, he decided to check in at the museum while the ladies finished in the kitchen.

The museum door was locked and marked Closed, but Amity spotted him and let him in. "Hello, Garrett. How may I help you today?"

Only a Finch would say "may" instead of "can."

Garrett walked around the museum picking up a new

brochure and noticing updated plaques about each display. "You've updated things a little."

"Oh, Keenan has helped me so much. I'll hate to see him go." She headed for the back door, where she prepared new displays. "You've got to see this."

Towers of boxes cluttered the room, including several donated from the Bailey mansion after last spring's remodeling. "I'm working on a display about our local authors— Aunt Anita, of course, and her uncle Wallace Tuttle. A couple of book collectors have asked me if I'm willing to sell. Of course not. But this is what I want to show you."

She took him to a five-foot-square table in the middle of the room, where light from a skylight and a window gave excellent light for work. What he saw intrigued him. He flipped through a stack of index cards, giving enough information to suggest the event: the Saint Albans Raid, the northernmost battle of the Civil War, when rebels robbed three banks and claimed the town for the Confederacy, and the copycat crimes in Maple Notch.

Someone had drawn a scale drawing of the exhibits, of Saint Albans, the road connecting the two towns, the inside of the bank, the original Tuttle Bridge—even the Reid family cave. So far the diorama had recognizable landscape, the hills and valleys, roads and rivers.

"Did Keenan do all this?" Garrett said. Whoever had planned this display had not only studied the subject but had an architect's approach and an artist's hand.

"Yes. Isn't it fantastic?" Amity took a card and read it, replacing it in the pile. "Are you here to ask about Keenan?"

"Why, can't I enjoy Maple Notch's best museum?"

"Our only museum, you mean, although the ice arena has a wonderful room honoring Vermont skaters."

Garrett chuckled. "Yes, I wanted to check on Keenan,

but I can tell he must have spent a lot of time on this project."

"He's worked more than the required hours. We've continued the studies of American history, but the diorama is his favorite activity."

Verity didn't finish with the tea shop as soon as she hoped, and when she went to the dining room, Garrett was gone.

"He said he'd be back in a few minutes," the server said. "His car is still out front."

Turning on her phone, Verity looked for Garrett's number. She should add him to her speed dial. Learning he was at the museum, she headed across the square, leaving her car at the tea shop's parking lot, as Garrett had done.

He had directed her to come in from the back door, and it opened before she could knock. "Come in. You won't believe what Keenan has done."

Panic seized Verity's heart, but Garrett sounded happy. He led her to a table in the middle of the room. "He did all of this."

Verity recognized the topography of Maple Notch and the cards with her son's neat handwriting. "He did? Why haven't I heard about it before?"

Amity looked at Garrett. "I asked the same question," he said.

"He wanted to keep it a secret, for Christmas. When he shows it to you, please act surprised."

"You seemed a little discouraged. I thought seeing what Keenan's been up to would help." Garrett scratched behind his ear. "Ms. Adams will have to see this, to assess Keenan's progress."

Amity frowned. "She's already called to make an appointment. I have sent her weekly reports of the material I've covered with Keenan, but she wants to give him a comprehensive test. She scares me, and I love history."

"Remember Mr. Nelson?" Verity asked.

Garrett nodded. "He was too busy coaching the football team to care about our own history. But since I was their star player—" he shrugged "—I didn't care."

"I didn't have Mr. Nelson for history," Amity said.

"He left a year after I graduated. After we won the state championship, he was recruited by a college program." Garrett waved his hand over the table. "This speaks well for Keenan. I'll be sure to report it in his file. But, Verity, you said you wanted to talk?"

Verity hesitated, not wanting to speak in front of Amity. Her sister seemed to understand. "I have some paperwork to finish in the office, if the two of you don't mind."

"That's all right, we were on our way out." Garrett held the door open. "Ladies first."

A man with such old-fashioned values and a commitment to making strong families had no business being single. Someday he might tell her why. A glance at his face, serious with no sense of humor, reminded her she was the mother of his client and nothing more. If she was single and childless, would he be interested in her? Her pulse quickened at the thought. But if any man could handle a wife with a ready-made family, Garrett was that man.

He said, "I gather that you want to talk privately. Where do you suggest we go?"

His voice was friendly, and she relaxed. "How about the park? It's a nice day." With sun overhead, the most recent snow gone from the ground, the cold air wasn't too bad with a winter coat. They walked across the frozen grass and took a seat on a wrought-iron bench—left there from the beginning of the last century and donated by one of their ancestors, no doubt.

"It's hard to find a place in town where we can talk without fear of my family overhearing, at least downtown." With the Bailey mansion/tea shop on one side of the town square, the museum on a second and the church they all attended on the third—lots of Finches rattled around the center of town.

"And you want an unofficial meeting." Garrett sounded totally neutral.

"Yes. No. I'm not sure." She threw her head back and looked at the sky, where a single cloud floated by. "Maybe I have nothing to worry about, after what I saw at the museum." She stopped speaking.

Garrett broke a short silence. "Are you asking for my professional opinion?"

She shrugged.

He said, "Keenan is doing well, although I'll keep my eye on him through the rest of the school year. Keep up whatever it is you're doing, and you should be fine."

"But I can't." The words burst from Verity's throat. "The doctor is moving and the office is closing. I'm out of a job by the end of the year."

Garrett stared ahead, his foot tapping the ground as if keeping up with his thoughts. "You were working at the tea shop this morning. Will you go back there to work?"

Verity shifted her hands up and down, weighing her answer. "For a couple of weeks. The cook is taking time off while his family is visiting over the holidays, and both the B and B and the tea shop are full up through the end of the year. Felicity's overbusy. But. Here's the problem." She drew in a deep breath. Garrett probably didn't know the details of everything her sister had done to help her through Mason's illness. "She shouldn't pay me. She paid me a full salary all that time last spring when I was at the hospital with Mason. I'm happy to help but…"

"You need to make money." Garrett nodded. "Do you think you need to work part-time because of Keenan?"

"It's complicated. Mason's too young to stay alone, and I don't want to jeopardize Keenan's progress by asking him to babysit." She leaned back against the chair and closed her eyes, tears pushing against her eyelids.

Garrett didn't jump in with meaningless reassurances. Instead, he said, "When do you need to make a decision?"

"By Christmas."

"Let me think about it and check out community resources at the office. As for you, why don't you brainstorm a list of everything you like to do. Look for the job you want, instead of whatever place offers you a job."

Could it be as easy as that? Looking into Garrett's smiling face, she believed it might be possible.

Chapter 8

Verity hated searching for a job. On Monday she called about everything she had noted when she checked the on-line job boards. On Tuesday she completed three applications. Two of the employers called her back for interviews. Both of them were full-time, the hours impossible with her situation.

By Thursday evening, exhaustion had set in, and Verity was fighting depression. While macaroni and cheese baked in the oven, she took stock of the contents of the cabinets. Not bad—she had quite a bit of food. So many people brought food when Mason was sick, she still hadn't used all the nonperishables. She could cut her grocery budget in half for a while, if need be.

The doorbell rang and Des answered. "It's Garrett."

Verity patted her hair and worried about her tatty-but-comfortable sweatshirt. "I didn't expect to see you tonight." The mac and cheese wouldn't feed five people. Maybe if she put together a salad…

"Sorry if I came at a bad time." Garrett held up a bundle of papers. "Here is the resource list I promised you. Where shall I put it?"

"Next to my computer." Verity came around the counter dividing dining room from living room. "Do you want to stay for supper?"

The room went silent at her question, but Garrett was already shaking his head. "I can't stay tonight. I'll call you later, in case you have questions. And can I look to seeing you at church again next Sunday?"

"We haven't decided." They said goodbye, and Verity stood at the door, watching Garrett run down the stairs to his car.

Frustration set in. Verity shut the doors to the cupboards with more force than necessary. They might have plenty of food, but not healthy, and not company-quality. The timer went off and she called the family to dinner.

Dinner helped Verity to relax, and she looked over homework. Keenan's brand of music played in the background—some of it wasn't so bad. Garrett's resource sheets could wait until tomorrow.

In the morning, she picked up the list more out of a sense of duty than with any hope. Today's priorities were data entry and another baking session with Felicity. She quickly realized the list was more extensive than the one Garrett had given her earlier. Garrett had pulled together resources for single parents, military families, psychologists who worked with teens, food banks. She chuckled. Maybe he had read her mind the other night. Other groups specialized with school supplies, including extracurricular activities. Tutors, too. The list ended with employment agencies: temporary positions, on-call agencies, even substitute teachers. That one he'd highlighted with a note. "You'd be great at this."

Verity shook her head, surprised. She had majored in secondary education in college, but had never completed student teaching and wasn't certified to teach. Between their moves and the children, she hadn't ever gone back. Getting certified now would take several steps, too time-consuming.

That was unfortunate since teaching hours would match the children's schedules.

It might be too late for her dreams, but not for her children's. Tomorrow Des would go ice skating. Who knew, perhaps another Olympian would spring from the family tree. Verity smiled at her bit of foolishness.

They hurried through their usual Saturday breakfast, munching on reheated waffles and leftover muffins with hot chocolate "because we're skating." Des took extra time in the bathroom. Such a lovely young woman, in black leggings perfect for the ice rink, her walnut-colored hair held back by a black headband and even a dash of makeup on her face.

Keenan fried an egg while he drank a cup of coffee. After he sat down, Verity asked, "What was your best time this week, Keenan?"

He held a piece of toast and egg an inch from his mouth. "Church last Sunday."

"I liked church, too, but my favorite thing was playing soccer at school." Mason frowned. "I wish I could skate today, too."

"I'll sign up for a family day before Christmas, if I can." But should she? Every expense, including holiday gifts, counted against the loss of income.

Verity stayed at the ice arena for a few minutes, long enough to notice the sideways glances boys were sending her daughter's way. Had the time already come to give her guidelines? Yes, for both of her teens.

While the youth skated, Verity took Mason to the nearest park for a game of catch. When they returned, Des was glowing, happier than Verity had seen her in a long time. She stayed on the ice, talking with other girls from the church.

Garrett skated to the side rail, fluid on ice, beautiful to watch. "Des had a great time. Have you ever considered skating classes for her?"

Lessons. "If I were a rich man." She hummed the tune from the musical *Fiddler on the Roof.*

"I could talk with the director. She is my cousin, after all." Garrett winked. "Keenan had fun, too."

Des pulled up beside Garrett before Verity had a chance to answer. "Mom, a group of kids are going to McDonald's for lunch. They invited me to go with them and they'll get me home." Keenan was skating their way. "Him, too."

Pleased that both of them were making friends, Verity pulled a bill from her dwindling stack of cash and handed it to her daughter. "Have fun, you two."

"See you tomorrow?" Garrett asked as he skated backward, still facing her.

"Yes." Verity waved goodbye. On the way out, she picked up a brochure about skating lessons. A glance told her private lessons at full cost could never happen. So much for dreams.

On the last day before Garrett's winter break, he closed his final case file with a smile. If every case went as well as Keenan's, Garrett would help truants until he died. But there was only one mother like Verity Clark, and he wished he could make her life easier.

Before he put the file away, he opened the pictures he

had scanned onto his computer from his time at the museum. In spite of the digital age, he left a paper trail in case questions arose later. Physical evidence aided discussions with teachers, counselors, parents and everyone else involved.

With the pictures printed and the file returned to the cabinet, Garrett prepared to leave. Before he could get out of his office, the phone rang. Caller ID indicated the high school, and he groaned. Probably a student had started his winter break early.

When he picked up the phone, the high school secretary said, "Mr. Sawtelle. I'm glad I caught you in the office."

Garrett didn't like the serious sound of her voice, not at all. "What happened?"

"We received a note from Ms. Adams that Keenan Clark missed class. That's his first class after the lunch period. There's no sign of him anywhere. I believe he left during lunch."

Garrett wrote down the information, thanked the secretary and drummed his fingers on the table. Verity would have told him if she had planned a trip. This was obviously Keenan's choice.

Garrett didn't need to let Verity know, not yet. He would check a few places on his own first. Start with the museum.

"Maple Notch Historical Museum," Amity answered.

"It's Garrett. Is Keenan scheduled to work this afternoon?" He held his breath, hoping the simplest explanation was true.

"No, he isn't. I'm closing early today myself, and keeping it closed until after the New Year."

For some kids, empty hours became the gateway to trouble of various kinds. Garrett thought some more and went into the outer office. "If I'm not back by three o'clock, go ahead and leave early."

"Is something wrong?" his assistant asked.

"I'll find out." He put on his coat. "Merry Christmas, to you and your family."

"Ditto, and Happy New Year to you," she said.

In spite of Garrett's forced smile, his heart remained heavy as he left the office. "Lord, help me find Keenan before he gets into trouble." All that Garrett knew about Keenan's hangouts was that Verity found him at the town's ball fields. Garrett would start there.

The fields, with two baseball diamonds, four soccer fields, one football field, as well as other sports, took up a hefty tract of land. Garrett drove around the perimeter without seeing anyone.

It was time to speak with Verity. He hated to do this to her. He held his phone in his hand, debating about whether to tell her in person, or to call ahead. His heart wanted to see her, to hold her, comfort her. But his head told him time was fleeting and they needed to find Keenan soon.

"He left school? At lunch!" Verity's voice went from calm to hysterical in five words.

Garrett cringed. "Yes. He's not at the museum or the park."

Verity cut a sob short. In the background, computer keys clacked. "I can't believe it." She sounded almost relieved.

"What?"

"If I am right about what he put on his social media, he took his driver's test this afternoon. I wonder who's been teaching him to drive. I kept putting him off…"

"Is he old enough?" Garrett calculated. Tenth grade. It depended on his birthday.

"He turned sixteen on Thanksgiving Day. I had no

idea… Wait a minute." A rap suggested she had laid the phone down. She came back in a minute. "Come over here. Now."

The midday roads were clear enough for Garrett to make it in minimum time. A vaguely familiar car sat next to Verity's vehicle.

The door opened as soon as Garrett knocked. "Come in. You have to hear it."

Keenan sat on the couch, his excitement over getting his license still making him oblivious to the trouble he was in.

The youth pastor from the Community Church stood a couple of feet from Verity, obviously disturbed. "Mr. Sawtelle, I had no idea of Keenan's problems. When he asked me to teach him how to drive, I was glad to help. Keenan swore he had permission to leave school for the test. He said he wanted to give his mother a Christmas present." He shrugged. "I should have asked. I am *so* sorry, Mrs. Clark."

Verity's foot was tapping quickly enough to beat a hole through a wooden floor, but her voice was even when she said, "No one's blaming you. If you don't mind, please leave, so I can discuss this with my son—and his truant officer."

They were in for a long afternoon. Garrett called the museum, gave Amity an update and asked her to pick up Des and Mason and keep them with her until further notice.

"I guess I thought they'd tell you later. After the break." That's what Keenan's mumbled words sounded like.

"And you think that would make it okay?" Verity's voice had gone cold.

"You weren't going to teach me. But you want my help. 'Keenan, take care of Mason while I go to Aunt Felicity's to help her bake.' 'Keenan, cook supper because I'll be home late.' 'Keenan, I know you want to play football, but I don't have time to take you to practice.' 'Keenan, even if you do learn how to drive, I can't afford the insurance.'" With each statement, his voice rose, until he was almost shouting. "But when I ask you to treat me like an adult, like to go to the movies with some friends, you act like I'm Mason's age."

Verity bit her tongue to keep her anger under control. "I can't believe this." He had done so well recently. What had him angry now? She wished she could go for a walk, to let go of her anger and ask God for wisdom and compassion and peace.

Keenan paced with the same restless energy, the two of them a pair of caged tigers.

Garrett didn't speak, waiting on the recliner, listening to the conversation, doing something with his phone. He could afford to be Keenan's friend. She couldn't. She was his parent. That made her angry at Garrett, and jealous, too, for the lack of connections that would hold him down.

When Keenan stopped pacing, he looked more resigned than angry.

Verity withdrew the angry accusations she wanted to spout and settled on a more neutral approach. "I'm ready to listen."

"If I could make a suggestion," Garrett said.

Both Keenan and Verity looked at him, grateful for his interruption.

"It might help to go to a neutral location. My church isn't far from here. They'll be happy to find a place for you—the church library is one of my favorite places for private conversations. Would you like me to call?"

Verity nodded her head while Keenan said, "Yes."

Satisfied, Garrett made the call. "They're expecting you."

When they reached the parking lot, Garrett went to his car. "Do you think you'll be at church on Sunday?"

Panicked, Verity realized that Garrett didn't expect to see her again before Sunday. "I don't know yet. But—" she looked at Keenan, and decided he had lost his right to veto her request "—can you come with us now? We both need to know what the consequences for this afternoon will be."

Garrett nodded. "I do need to talk with you about it, but it doesn't have to be today."

Keenan relaxed, and Verity's anger riled again. Garrett was playing the part of the good parent, delaying any serious discussion. She had to take Keenan home tonight, decide on immediate consequences and make him feel like she had ruined his Christmas break.

Christmas. She was in no mood for Christmas right this minute, but God's love hadn't changed because of her bad day.

Not looking at either Garrett or Verity, Keenan said, "I'd like you to be there."

Garrett looked at both of them. "I'll meet you there, then."

Keenan didn't speak while they drove to the church, and Verity was glad. She couldn't handle small talk. It was a good thing Garrett had already arranged for Amity to stay with Des and Mason. Who knew how long mother and son would need to settle things?

The pastor met them at the door and led them to the church library. "Would you care for coffee? Soda, maybe?"

They gave him their preferences. He returned before Garrett arrived. Keenan took the soda can with him as he scanned the books in the library. Verity didn't bother. Today's visit wasn't meant to encourage Keenan's reading habits.

Keenan sat down across from Verity. "All they seem to have are sappy love stories and books about the Bible."

"One of the bulletins reviewed a book, part of a series, about an FBI agent. It sounded kind of like one of those TV shows. You can ask about it later."

"If I still have time to read."

"That might be all you get to do for fun." Verity meant the words to be light, but they came out as a threat.

Garrett took a seat between them, a buffer that made Verity feel more at ease.

"Give me the lowdown, Garrett," Keenan said. "Are you ready to kick me out of school?"

Chapter 9

Garrett weighed his words—Keenan had to take the consequences seriously. "No. In fact, you have detention every day of your first week of school. If you missed any assignments or tests today, you'll receive a big, fat zero, and it will count against your final grade."

Keenan relaxed. He probably knew, as Garrett did, that no teacher planned serious work the final few hours before the winter break. None of the teachers was that much of a Grinch.

Before Keenan could celebrate, Garrett said, "This is what upsets me the most. If you had stuck out those last few hours, the school would have considered you as a student in good standing. You would have been eligible for any extracurricular activities."

Keenan shrugged. "It's already way too late for basketball."

Garrett leaned forward. "What about baseball—in the

spring?" Keenan couldn't hide the light in his eyes before he looked away.

Garrett continued relentlessly. "The season starts up in a few months, but you might still be on probation. You have to stay on your toes and not mess up again."

Keenan sat back against the chair, as if he didn't have a worry in the world. "What about history? Can I keep working at the museum?"

"I'm waiting for Ms. Adams's assessment of your term paper." Garrett expected the teacher to give Keenan high marks, but Keenan didn't need to know that. "You have problems at school, and I'll work with you. But your mother decides what happens at home."

Verity was tapping her fingernails on the side table loud enough to join a band. "Before I say anything, I want to hear your side of the story." She took a long drag of coffee, emptying the cup. Her hard-won composure impressed Garrett.

The silence stretched out, and Garrett decided to prod the lion in the cage. "You didn't answer your mother's question."

Keenan paced, stopping a foot away from his mother, staring down at her as if to intimidate. "I used to skip so I would have time to think about things. And I was learning how to drive."

Garrett hadn't heard the first explanation before. His confusion was mirrored on Verity's face. She said, "And you had to skip school to find time to sit and think?"

"Mom." Keenan made it into two syllables. "I never have any time alone at home. I share a room with my kid brother. The only way I can get any peace is to listen to music, and then you yell at me. If I stay up late, you get on my case."

Verity shrank into the chair back, and Keenan moved closer, crowding her.

"Des and I never saw you when Mason was sick. He's better now, but nothing else has changed. You're working at the tea shop over Christmas, and you want me to spend all my days on babysitting duty."

Verity bared her teeth but she didn't speak.

"I need to be alone sometimes." Keenan's intensity almost made the bookshelves shiver. He drew back and took a seat. In a normal voice, he said, "And so what if I missed a couple of useless classes to get my driver's license?"

Verity hadn't said a word. Garrett prayed that she would find the strength, empathy, wisdom to respond.

She straightened in her chair. "Keenan—this has been hard on all of us."

Lord, keep her strong.

Keenan's face grew red enough for a stroke.

"But I haven't seen it from your side." She looked at Garrett, her face resolute, apology written in the lines around her eyes. "Because you're my oldest, the most responsible, I leaned on you. Maybe too much." She stood. When she took a step forward, Keenan stood, as well. They met in the middle. "I am so proud of you, of the man you are becoming, of all the hundreds of ways you have helped me since your father died. I'm even glad you managed to get your driver's license."

She put her hands on his shoulders. Keenan trembled, not speaking.

"What makes me feel even worse is that I know what it's like to be the oldest child, the responsible one." A single tear trickled from her right eye, followed by one from her left. "And then I made the same mistakes with you. I'm so sorry, Keenan." Tears cascaded down her face.

"Mom." Keenan put his arms around his mother. Garrett walked away to find the box of tissues that the library kept on hand.

When the tears stopped and Verity stepped away from Keenan, Garrett handed her a box of tissues. When she tried to thank him, she hiccuped instead of speaking. Her hiccup turned into a laugh, and then she laughed as hard as she had cried.

Most men ran away when a woman acted so hysterical. Garrett stood a few feet away, observing her like a rat in a maze. She caught the laughter before it threatened to start her crying again. "Thank you, more than words can say."

The worried look on Keenan's face fled, but he stayed at a cautious distance from his mother.

Verity wanted to reassure him. "We're not done, but this was a good start."

Keenan crossed his arms. More than anything, she wished she didn't have to prod those tender spots again. "As much as I'd prefer to ignore our problems, we can't. I understand—better—why you left school today. But that doesn't change the problems we face, and there must be consequences."

He frowned, but kept his eyes on her.

"I wish we could put this discussion off. But we can't. I need the work—we need the money. If I put Mason with a babysitter, that takes a big chunk out of the money I make." Her voice wobbled. "I can't afford it."

"I suppose I could…" Keenan said.

"I have a suggestion." Garrett drew closer, forming a circle with the two of them. "More of an offer than a suggestion. I happen to have most of the next two weeks off." He grinned, a look on his face that made Verity happy inside. "Except for a couple of commitments I can't get out of."

"Christmas." Verity hiccuped again. She wanted to laugh at the funny expression that crossed Garrett's face, but kept silent.

"Hmm. I didn't think about that. Are you working at the B and B on Christmas Day?"

Verity nodded. Good for business, bad for family.

"Well, if you leave the tea shop at your usual time, I can even manage Christmas."

Keenan grinned like the Cheshire cat. "You would do that for me?"

"Not everything is all about you. I want to help your mother, as well," Garrett said.

Verity said, "Are you offering to take care of Mason over the Christmas break?"

Garrett nodded. "If you are willing."

Light-headed, Verity felt for the chair and sat. "Do you babysit for all your clients' families?" As soon as the words came out, she shook her head. Of course not. For some reason, Garrett had always taken a special interest in Keenan's case. In her inner dreams, which she hardly allowed a voice, she thought he was interested in her, too.

"I wish I could." Amusement mixed with shame played over his face. "But let me borrow your family for a few days, since so far God hasn't given me one of my own." A wistful note entered his voice as well as his face.

Maybe he did wish he had a family of his own. Verity silently cheered.

Garrett said, "I mean it, even about Christmas morning. If they will have me."

He didn't know what he was in for. Mason would be awake before she left for the tea shop, demanding to open his presents. "Actually, they're going to stay with Dad and enjoy our Christmas morning breakfast bonanza. And we've always opened our presents on Christmas Eve." Her heart pinged at the image of sitting at home, with Garrett dressed in a Santa Claus suit, ho-ho-hoing. She pushed the thought away.

Both Keenan and Garrett looked like she had tempted them with a three-layer cake before snatching it away. Garrett recovered first, rubbing his hands together. "Very well. When do you need me there tomorrow?"

Still not quite sure what had happened, she made the arrangements. As she and Keenan got into the car, she realized they hadn't chosen consequences for Keenan's lapse. Nonetheless, she felt more at peace than she had in a long time.

On Monday, Keenan and Des slept past Verity's alarm. Anxious to see Garrett, Mason joined her as soon as her feet hit the floor. When the phone rang, Verity had a second's panic that Garrett couldn't make it.

It was a wrong number.

Garrett arrived ten minutes before she had asked him to, walking in while she loaded the dishwasher. Life with teenagers and restaurant work didn't go well together. They stayed up late at night, keeping her awake until all her chicks were in bed, and then she had to arrive at the tea shop in time to serve breakfast to large groups of people by half past six.

Garrett handed her a cup of coffee. "One cream, if I remember right. I'm sorry it's not the real thing."

"I can fix that." She went to her refrigerator and poured a smidgeon of cream from Sawtelle's Organic Dairy.

"Thank you again. For everything. I wish I could do something to repay you," Verity said as Garrett helped her put on her coat.

"There is. Keep up the good work with Keenan."

Verity laughed, self-conscious. She didn't feel like she had done well with Keenan at all.

"But seriously, there is one thing you can do for me, and all it will cost is a little bit of time. Come with me tomorrow night. Just you and me, driving around to look at the Christmas lights."

Was he asking her on...a date? "But Mason..."

"Keenan offered to take care of him for a few hours, when I told him what I had in mind."

He must have asked Keenan sometime over the weekend, and her son hadn't said a word about it. Her heart sped at his invitation. So many years had passed since she met Curtis, so many years since she'd been on a date. She felt like a high schooler being asked to the prom.

"I love seeing the lights. Yes, I accept."

Garrett fiddled in front of the mirror. Why he worried, he didn't know. Verity had known him when he was a gangly ten-year-old, before he was the hometown football hero. Maybe that was the problem. He had kept in good shape, but he wasn't football-ready any longer.

Forget about it. He put on his favorite sweater and threw his coat in the backseat when he went out to the car, in case they decided to walk around.

Verity looked radiant, a cheery red sweater peeking above the collar of her dark blue coat, the few gray hairs sparkling like silver in the light over the door. A moonlit sky would be perfect, but heavy clouds overhead and the sudden drop of temperature suggested bad weather was in the offing. He satisfied himself with holding on to her arm, to make sure she didn't fall.

After he held the door for her to get in the car, he slipped behind the wheel. His plans for the evening depended in part on the weather.

"We can start here. The office sponsors a contest every year, and some residents go all out." She sighed. "If I can get tree lights shining through the window, I figure I've done enough."

Garrett thought of the tabletop tree in his own place, satisfied to enjoy his parents' tall tree, covered with the ornaments gathered over a lifetime. He glanced at Verity, wondering what it would be like to share a lifetime with a woman like her.

"This one is my favorite." Verity leaned across him, pointing to the left. He fought to ignore her closeness and instead sought out the apartment in question. In addition to the expected lights outlining the windows, bright stars hung suspended over life-size figurines of Mary and Joseph. Homemade bows hung around the lights.

A single snowflake settled on the windshield, melting as soon as it hit the glass. Before it got worse, Garrett wheeled the car out of the apartment complex and took the long way to the town square.

"I see lights down that way." Verity sounded as excited as a child, and Garrett turned down the street. They found a cul-de-sac with houses from the Edwardian era, decorated to suit.

Santa Claus sat outside one house, his red suit protecting him from the snow. His call of "Merry Christmas" penetrated the windows. He waved at them as they slowed for the show. Verity plastered her nose to the window.

"Want to talk to Santa Claus?" Garrett asked as he stopped the car.

She reached for the door handle, and Garrett ran around the car to open it for her. This time, he didn't hesitate, taking her hand in his as they walked to the waiting Santa Claus.

When they approached, Mrs. Claus came out with two

steaming cups of hot cocoa. Santa handed them each a peppermint stick to stir it with. Traffic by the house was slow, which surprised Garrett. Close up, he saw that it was the pastor of the Community Church, and his wife.

"Pastor Tuttle, I didn't know you were Santa Claus," Verity said.

"We pass it around the neighborhood. This year was our turn."

Verity sipped the cocoa as if uncertain what to say. The Tuttles, bless them, weren't probing. "We've been visiting the church where Garrett attends, and we're thinking about transferring our membership."

Santa looked from Verity to Garrett, his assessment uncomfortable. Then he smiled, and all of them relaxed. "Any church that preaches the Word of God is our sister in Christ. If that if the direction God leads you, I pray for blessings on you and the church."

"Thank you." Verity stirred the cocoa with the peppermint stick, before removing it and sucking the cocoa from the bottom of the stick. "What are you staring at?" she asked Garrett.

"You." He took his peppermint stick and did the same thing. "It tastes pretty good." He tipped his head back and let the chocolaty-minty syrup slide into his mouth.

They chatted as they finished the cocoa. After Mrs. Claus took the cups back into the house, Pastor Tuttle handed them a pamphlet. "You two already know the reason for the season, as they say. God gave the earth His Son to save us from our sin. As you go about this season, share that good news."

"Amen." They said their goodbyes and got back in the car. Snowflakes fell steadily, a feather-soft blanket covering land, homes and passing cars. Even the simplest of lights twinkled like stars in the sky through the glimmering snowfall.

"Let's go downtown," Verity said. "I'm there every morning, but I haven't seen it after dark this season." She chuckled. "My life has changed a lot over the past year."

"For the better?" He felt his eyebrow rise, the way it often did when he asked a question that perplexed him.

"Mostly. Last year, we drove through downtown every time we went to the hospital. I could tell you every display between our house and the hospital. Mason pointed every time he saw lights. I didn't take the kids this year, as it reminded me too much of those bad memories."

"It sounds like you made the best of a frightening experience. Mason will remember the lights after he has forgotten the runs to the hospital."

"Do you really think so?" Verity turned her attention from the window to Garrett.

He took her hand in his, squeezed and let it go, to keep his hands on the wheel. "I'm sure of it."

They drove across the bridge—highlighted with blue and green lights—and drove into the center of Maple Notch, the town square. "Do you mind if we get out and walk?"

Perfect. Garrett left his gloves in the car, and took Verity's hand in his as they skirted the west side of the square, by the town hall. "I feel like I'm in an ice palace."

Garrett agreed. In the glowing white lights, he could make out individual snow crystals. The exterior of the building shimmered with lights wrapped around every ridge and column, and a manger scene stood on the lawn. "I'm glad no one has complained about putting up the manger scene. That's happening all over the country these days."

"Yes. It's perfect."

Verity wasn't looking at the town hall—but at him. His heart warmed, working its way from the inside out. He leaned forward, she met him halfway, and he claimed her lips in a kiss.

Chapter 10

Preparing for the Christmas Eve service twenty-four hours later, Verity's lips still tingled with the memory of Garrett's kiss. No kiss—no man—had made her feel that way since Curtis. The thought scared her and excited her in equal measure.

"Mom, we're late." Mason stretched her name out, his arms across his chest. The adult pose made her laugh.

"Mom." He stretched her name out even longer. "Keenan's still eating."

"I'm done." Keenan dropped his trash in the can and rinsed off his plate before putting it in the dishwasher. That simple act was as good a present as anything sitting under the tree.

Verity took another look at her sage-green sweater with a spattering of gold across the yoke, her lightly made-up face, and decided she looked good enough. Des was dressed in a sweatshirt with fun Christmas cats. Mason had dressed in blue jeans and green shirt at the request of the children's choir director.

After they piled into the car, Verity said, "So, tell me about Garrett's aunt Hazel." Keenan had shoveled her sidewalk and driveway at Garrett's request.

Keenan rolled his head back against the headrest on the bucket seat. "Nice. A big place—I didn't know if I would finish shoveling in time." A smile flashed across his face. "I liked the pay."

"I'm proud of you, finding those jobs shoveling snow. People may call you all winter long."

"I hope so." Keenan looked at her. "If you let me."

Verity had grounded him. Church. School. Museum. Nothing else, not even extra activities at church. But he was going crazy without anything to do at home, a situation which could create more problems than it solved. And having some money of his own was a good thing, wasn't it?

"Until school starts, it will be okay. After that, I don't know." She paused. "I remember my first job. It was like a dream come true. I saved enough money to buy a computer." She had wanted a car.

Cars. She gulped. Now that he had his license, how long before he asked to borrow the car? Or to get his own car?

She dropped Mason off at the door, and he ran for the entrance. He had been in Christmas programs before, but she had rarely seen him so excited.

"Do you guys want to get out here? I'll have to park far away." The parking lot was full, as if a lot of guests had come to enjoy the Christmas pageant.

Des and Keenan got out, but before Verity could pull away to park, Garrett appeared. "May I park your car, ma'am?" He bowed as if he was a paid valet.

Laughing, she handed him the keys, then went inside, hung up her coat and waited for Garrett. Des and Keenan met up with the youth group seconds before Garrett walked through the door. "May I join you tonight?" He smiled, as if certain of her answer.

Nodding, she headed for the sanctuary doors on the right side. The pews were packed, and they had to walk halfway down the aisle before they spotted a place to sit. "It will be a tight fit when Mason joins us after the children sing."

Garrett winked. "I don't mind tight quarters."

A few minutes later, the service started. When they sang "Silent Night, Holy Night," Verity's mind went to last night, to the beauty of kissing under the snowy night, and warmth flooded her cheeks. Garrett looked at her sideways and squeezed her hand. Verity's heart flip-flopped.

Two children's choirs sang. The preschoolers were as adorable as always, a boy with bright red hair singing at the top of his out-of-tune voice, and half of them looking around, scared, at all the people in front of them.

Compared to them, Mason acted like a little adult. He stood straight in place, his eyes fixed on the director seated on the front pew. Around Verity, she saw parents, their heads touching as they leaned together, celebrating this special moment. Did it interest members with no connection to the children? Garrett smiled as they sang, his eyes catching every nuance of the performance. At least one member was interested. Or did his interest stem from his commitment to Verity and her children? His hand holding hers added spice to the moment.

Down the pew, a father was filming the performance on his phone. She should have invited her family to today's service, or at least thought to film it.

When the children finished, Garrett clapped. His eyes looked almost dewy.

He wanted children. It showed in every movement of

his face, every movement of his body. He was so good with children.

Mason squeezed in between them. "I did good."

"You sure did, son."

He's not your son. Verity fought to tie her emotions to reality. In happy fantasies, Garrett would meld into her family seamlessly. The sad truth was, no matter how much either one of them might want it, he was a friend, nothing more. At least, not today.

When it came time for the offering, Garrett bent over Mason's head. "Watch this."

The pastor called Keenan's friend Aaron to the mic before they passed the plates. The other youth, including Des and Keenan, crowded around him. "This year, we challenged ourselves to raise enough money to build an orphanage in Africa. We gave up some fun things—like a day at the amusement park last summer—but we made our goal. It's all in this jar."

Keenan and couple of boys stepped forward with a gigantic glass jug filled with coins and bills. Verity couldn't imagine how much they had raised, or how hard it was. The proud look on Keenan's face told her he had contributed, as well.

The ushers accepted the jug amid a standing ovation from the congregation. When the noise settled down, Aaron handed the mic to Keenan.

"What's Keenan gonna say?" Mason asked.

Verity shushed him, not wanting to miss a word. Even before he spoke, pride poured over Verity. Her son was barely sixteen, already taller than many of the other youth and a leader in whatever came next.

"I don't exactly know what to say. My name is Keenan Clark. I'm new to this church—moved back to Maple

Notch not long ago, although my mom's family has lived here forever."

Laughter rippled across the auditorium, and a few glances were sent Verity's way.

"But we wanted to do more than give money to someone far away. We wanted to do something ourselves, in person. So tomorrow, we're going to serve Christmas dinner at the Community Church."

Applause broke out before Keenan finished speaking. "That is, if our parents say yes. How about it, Mom?" He looked straight at her.

"Go ahead." Garrett smiled.

She stood. "I can't think of a better way to spend Christmas. And maybe we can bake a few extra muffins to send over for the dinner."

Laughter broke out, and the congregation stood to voice their approval.

Almost an hour later, they lit candles while they sang "Joy to the World!" By the time they walked out, Christmas Day had begun.

Garrett walked them to the car. "I'll be there before long."

Verity leaned on the car while the children piled in. "I don't know if I can sleep tonight."

He touched her cheek gently. "Sleep, if you can. Tomorrow—today—will be a long day."

Christmas week had been special, recorded memories Garrett knew he would replay many times. Most of all, he had grown used to seeing Verity every day when she came home from work. Tonight she had invited him to come back in the evening for a New Year's Eve celebration.

"Garrett's here." Mason closed the door and raced through the house. "Mom."

Verity came out of the bathroom, her hair freshly washed, light makeup highlighting her features, a silvery sweatshirt bringing life to her face. "Thank you for coming."

He wanted to kiss her cheek, but knew better, the same way he had avoided mistletoe whenever they were together with the kids. Tonight, perhaps, the children might begin to see them as a couple.

A father? He gulped. He hoped he was ready, but were they? And was Verity really ready for a new man in her life?

"We ate a light supper," Verity said. "I'm ordering pizza. What do you like?"

Garrett answered, "Pepperoni," immediately, and Mason cheered. Keenan came through, high-fived his brother and welcomed Garrett. While Verity called for pizza delivery, Garrett took Keenan aside. "Can you give me a couple of minutes, for some grown-up talk? We'll be finished in plenty of time for the pizza. I promise."

Des huffed but went to her room. Mason's shoulders heaved as if the world weighed on his shoulders, but he settled down in a far corner of the living room, building with his favorite Christmas present.

Keenan straightened in his chair, pulling himself to his full height. Verity stayed in the kitchen, accepting Garrett's hint.

This apartment wasn't designed for private conversations, but Garrett pulled a chair up so he and Keenan sat almost knee to knee. From the briefcase he carried, he extracted a single sheet from Keenan's file. "This is my recommendation to your school regarding your latest absence." Only hard effort kept his face stern. He would let the words speak for themselves.

Closing his eyes, Keenan took the letter. Praying or

gathering his courage, Garrett guessed. When Keenan read the first line, he smiled, and when he reached the end, he pumped his fist in the air. "Yes!"

Mason looked up before returning to his play. Verity poked her head around the corner but stayed put.

"Consider it a belated Christmas present. No, it's not a present. You earned it," Garrett said.

Keenan jumped up. "Mom, you've got to see this."

Verity didn't wait for a second invitation. She joined them in the living room. "Good news?"

"It's all here. Garrett lists all sorts of stuff. Here, read it for yourself."

As Verity read the letter, Garrett reviewed his suggestions. Of his own volition, Keenan had given sacrificially to help strangers build an orphanage in Africa. He had served Christmas dinner to the needy of Maple Notch. He had shoveled snow for the homebound and disabled, when heavy snows fell in time for Christmas. He had promised to return every time it snowed throughout the winter.

The doorbell rang, and Keenan opened the door to the pizza delivery driver, and Verity finished reading the letter before paying him. "In light of all the actions Keenan Clark has done on behalf of others, without any expectation of return, I recommend that he be restored to normal status, able to participate in extracurricular activities, under the same restrictions put in place last November." Verity ran to Garrett and hugged his neck before kissing him on the cheek.

Garrett stumbled back a step, breaking the embrace, but he hadn't moved soon enough. Des had poked her head out of the door when the pizza arrived. Verity pulled back, her cheeks red, and she hunted through her purse for the cash. "Forget it, I'll use the credit card."

The driver couldn't accept her card—credit card deliveries had to be given at the time of the order—and Verity had to empty her purse to locate the money she needed. Garrett offered to pay, but she refused. The tussles gave her a few minutes to recover from her embarrassment.

The driver accepted the money with a generous tip and left.

Des had disappeared. As Mason and Keenan poured drinks and took their seats, Verity went to the bedroom and came out alone.

"She's not hungry." Verity closed her lips, deflecting any unspoken questions, and joined them at the table.

Garrett looked at the door and thought about speaking to Des. He thought they had a good relationship. Not good enough, apparently, to see her mother kiss him.

Garrett had run into this problem before. Most of the Christian singles his age had been married, and those marriages had ended either in divorce or death. Dating mothers came with the responsibility of winning the children's approval, as well.

Obviously he had a long way to go.

Verity saw the hurt on Garrett's face, the pain sketched in lines around his mouth, his determination to make it right. She shook her head. "Give her time."

If she had hoped tonight the children could see Garrett as someone other than Keenan's truant officer, more even than a family friend, her plan had backfired. Garrett returned thanks for the food, and the boys dived in as if they hadn't eaten all day. The meat pizzas disappeared quickly, and Verity was glad she had ordered a third, all-veggie pizza designed to appeal to Des's palate.

Garrett and Mason played Battleship while Keenan surfed through the channels. Verity slipped away, with two pizza slices, diet soda with little ice and a pair of cinnamon bread sticks. Des sat on her top bunk, legs crossed, reading her Bible.

Verity put one foot on the ladder and knocked the wood. "Permission to enter? I bear food."

When Des didn't answer, Verity climbed to the top bunk. Des scooted over to give her mother room to sit. She tucked her Bible under her pillow and munched on the pizza. When she finished, she sucked the last of the cinnamon sugar from her fingers and inched closer to her mother. Leaning forward, she stared into her face. "Are you and Garrett dating?"

The temptation to dissemble hit Verity in the throat. One night didn't qualify as dating. Did it? "We had one date." She didn't elaborate.

"You kissed him. I saw you."

"He brought us good news about Keenan. I kissed him on the cheek. I was just saying thank you."

Des just looked at her. "You don't kiss my teachers when you thank them."

"You're right. I wasn't thinking. I treated him like... family."

"But he's not family. And he never will be. No one can ever take Dad's place." Des nodded with conviction, her conclusion irrefutable.

Did Des expect Verity to never marry again? Verity had never given them reason to think she might. "Your father was a special man, someone I loved very much. But tonight Garrett is our guest, and I expect you to treat him with kindness. I want us to see the New Year in as a family."

Shrugging, Des jumped off the bed. "It's okay. I'll be back." She headed for the bathroom.

Once in the living room, Verity sat cross-legged on the floor beside Mason, who was staring at his screen. "Garrett won the last game."

"Maybe if I help you, we'll win."

Grinning, Mason scooted over and allowed her closer to the screen. Garrett rubbed his hands together. "I've got my work cut out for me."

Keenan glanced up, his attention quickly returned to the football game on the TV. The sound of running water came from the bathroom.

"I move first," Garrett said. "Winner's right." The place he called was at the top right corner, a miss.

Mason's first call hit a ship, and soon they had sunk Garrett's biggest ship. By then, Garrett had found one of their ships, and quickly sunk it. They raced through the game. "We won, Mom!"

"We make a good team." Verity hugged her son.

"I bet I could beat you." Des stood at the doorway, hair still damp from her shower, face devoid of the makeup she enjoyed wearing so much these days. "Do you mind?"

"Of course not." Garrett relinquished his spot. He and Verity sat on the couch at the same time. "Do you remember when I asked you what you thought you would like to do to make money?" he said in a low voice the kids couldn't overhear.

"Naturally." Every second of their single date had created a memory, one she didn't think she would ever forget.

"Do you have an answer?"

Keenan had earbuds in his ears, Des and Mason were playing the game. No one was paying close attention.

"Let me show you." Going to her desk, Verity brought her laptop back to the couch and opened to her blog. "I blog once a week, a hodgepodge of sorts, about life in rural New England, about raising three children as a single mom, about military families— although I don't do that much anymore. At first I spilled my guts, a journal where I could vent my feelings. I've got about five hundred people reading my blog every week."

She propped her chin on her hand. "I wonder if I can find a way to make money with it. Then I think that's a stupid idea. Look at all the problems I've had with Keenan. What do I know?"

Garrett shook his head. "Vulnerability. Nobody wants to listen to a know-it-all." Touching her computer, he said, "May I?"

She nodded, and he took the computer onto his own lap. He scanned the page quickly, hit keys to follow links elsewhere, and his expression hardly changed. After several minutes, he blew out his breath and sat back in his seat. "A-ma-zing. Your posts are well-written—maybe you inherited the family writing gene."

"I doubt that. Aunt Anita's books are still required reading in Vermont schools." Verity laughed. "Felicity is the one with a story to tell, how she met Travis through that TV show and all the decisions they had to make about putting Aunt Anita into a rest home."

"Don't be so quick to doubt yourself. Felicity may have the fairy tale. But you write about real life, problems everyone can relate to. I can see why people read your blog, and I know there must be ways to make money."

"But you don't know how." Verity filled in the gap. "But Felicity does. Her website for the B and B is generating a lot of income." She waited a moment. "I've also thought about that degree and becoming a teacher."

"Mom, Garrett—play with me, please." Mason slid the lid off a wooden box that replicated a game from her grandparents' time.

"Sure. As long as I can be the colonel." Garrett fondled an imaginary mustache.

As the minutes counted down to midnight, they stood

on the porch to watch the fireworks. Keenan found the radio station that broadcast the music that matched the light show. Des danced in time with the music, and Mason jumped around.

Garrett and Verity stood back, as close as they could be without touching. She wished she could lean her head on his shoulder, his arm around her. Instead, she followed through on their earlier discussion. "Turnabout is fair play. What are your dreams for the future?"

Chapter 11

Garrett's future dreams stood next to him. He could see himself as Verity's husband, a father to her children, enjoying simple evenings like this New Year's Eve. But he didn't dare say those hopes aloud.

He put it in broader terms. "I want the same things most men want. To make a difference. To build something lasting. A family. Love. Pretty ordinary stuff."

Silvery flecks sparkled in her eyes when he mentioned family and love. He didn't dare say any more. Not now, not here where her children could overhear every word.

"Those are good dreams. And you are already making a difference. Think of all the children and families you help."

A firework exploded, delaying Garrett's answer. "I wish. I might make a difference ten percent of the time, twenty percent if I'm lucky. If I could reverse the trends, succeed ninety percent of the time—or even fifty-one percent—I'd be happy."

"You sound like Rudyard Kipling's poem *If*. 'You'll be a man, my son!'" She smiled.

"I guess."

Another boom sent up a spectacular splash of yellow and red.

"Look at that display. It's beautiful. But will we remember it a year from now? I won't. Don't worry so much about the ones who get away. Think about the ones you do help." She spread her arms to encompass the horizon. "We are here today because our ancestors carved a home out of the wilderness. I'm sure they made mistakes, but they built a strong foundation. I hope—you hope—that children a hundred years from now will thrive because of the work we do today."

"By God's grace."

"Exactly. To a thousand generations. That's God's promise."

The sparkles died away, and an orchestra played the introduction to another song on the radio. Mason's nose wrinkled. "What's that?"

The music sounded familiar to Garrett, but he couldn't place the melody. Des tapped her right foot, moving in time to the music. "It's the state song."

Before she finished speaking, a chorale sang, "'These green hills and silver waters.'" Multiple rockets flew into the sky, exploding in a burst of green and silver and gold, all the words of the song, as well as the red of the sugar maple, red clover and monarch butterfly, all symbols of Vermont. A final burst of greens and blues shaped like Mount Mansfield exploded as the chorale finished the song. "'These green mountains are my home.'"

Des sang along with the music, a lovely soprano that fell pleasantly on the ear. When she got to high school, she belonged in a choir. If she enjoyed music, she might like marching band, as well.

"Des, do you play any instruments?" he asked as the music died away.

Mouth closed as if she hadn't sung a word, she shook her head.

Verity looked at him, puzzled.

"I was thinking about the marching band in high school. Choir, too."

Des watched the last colors flutter to the ground before she turned around. "Why do you care? You're not my father." She slipped between them into the living room and settled in front of the television.

"Des." Verity moved, but Garrett held her back, shaking his head.

The night he had hoped to enjoy as a stress-free time with the Clark family had turned into a disaster, and the bell had rung on the New Year. Garrett decided to leave. "I pray you have a blessed new year, everyone. I'll see you tomorrow."

Verity walked him to the door. "I apologize for Des."

He shook his head. "Don't. She's entitled to her feelings."

"But not to be rude." Verity's lips thinned, her shoulders sagged, but she managed a small smile. "Thank you for coming today. I'm only sorry it had to end this way."

"It happens." With Des staring at them from the door to her bedroom, Garrett felt no temptation to hug his hostess, let alone kiss her again. "Thank you for a fun evening. Don't let a few bad moments ruin the celebration."

"Thank you. Again."

Garrett arrived at his apartment a few minutes later. He checked the messages that had arrived on his phone during the evening. Mom and Dad, safely retired to Florida, wished him well: "Wish you were here." Every other year or so, he traveled south to spend a week with his folks. They couldn't understand why their one unmarried offspring didn't always want to spend the holidays with his parents. His cousin Nick had called, as well.

Garrett couldn't settle down to sleep. In spite of his reassurances to Verity, Des's behavior upset him. She was rude, but he had experienced that before with his clients. His heart broke because if Verity's children rejected him, he didn't stand a chance with their mother.

Garrett picked up his Bible and removed the index card passed out during the service last Sunday. The pastor had challenged the congregation to ask God for His dreams for them.

Garrett had waited until he reached His house and found only one dream that captured his heart. He had pressed his pen down so hard that it almost cut through the card: Verity. After tonight, more than ever, the dream was only possible if God intervened.

Save a boy from getting expelled from school. Save his sister from heading down the same path. Convince their mother that a bachelor of his age was good marriage material and shower her with abundant expressions of love.

Garrett closed his eyes. If not Verity, maybe this year he would meet someone else, the woman God had for him. The problem was, whenever he listed the qualities he wanted in a woman, like warmth, sincerity, faithfulness, Verity's face swam before his eyes.

Eyes wide-open, he talked with God about it. "Since You're my Abba Father, I know You want what is best for me. Whether I remain single or married, or whichever woman You have for me—if I can trust You for eternal life, I can trust You with this life."

* * *

Verity had applied for a position as a substitute teacher the day before winter break, and she received a call the first day school started again in the new year. A pregnant teacher had been put on bed rest; the position was Verity's for several months. God was so good; no need for child care, since her hours matched the kids'.

Des's outburst on New Year's Eve made Verity decide to join the single-parents group at church. Others must deal with introducing new relationships to their kids. How would she describe her children's reactions to Garrett? Mason adored him, Keenan respected him, but Des rejected him.

Monday evening, Verity sat down with the kids. "I'm going to be at church tomorrow night." Amid the not-church-again groans, she said, "Keenan and Des, you can stay home. You can either finish your homework before supper, or I can check it when I get home. And, Mason, you get to come with me."

Mason grinned until Verity said, "You'll be in a child care group the church provides. I'm going to a class for single parents."

No one seemed to know what to say. "So you can complain about all of us?" Keenan's joke held a hint of pain.

"I don't know what they do at the meetings. I've heard they read books and talk and have fun. We might exchange ideas about what works."

In spite of Keenan's progress, he continued to worry her. He was a loner, and sometimes loners ended up with the wrong friends. What had happened to his friends from middle school? Question number one to ask at the group: how to keep track of your teen's friends without acting like a spy.

"Do we have to go tonight, Mom?" Mason asked as they drove to church on Tuesday night. "I'd rather be at home."

Tired as Verity was after a day of teaching, she couldn't disagree. "It's important. I want to be a better mother, and this will help."

"You're already the best, Mom." Mason punched her arm as she pulled into the church parking lot.

His improved mood disappeared when they walked to the children's room. He stopped at the door and frowned. "They're all little kids."

Verity wondered if their parents were young, as well, but she took Mason's hand and walked in. The caretaker was an older woman, Mary Roberts. Her warm smile set Verity's mind at ease. "And you must be Mason. I can tell you'll be a big help for me tonight."

Mason's face brightened and Mary winked at Verity as they walked farther into the room.

She found her way to the room where the single-parents group met. "Verity, I was so glad when I heard you were coming tonight." A man a little younger than her welcomed her. He wore a wedding ring. Was he married or, like her, wearing a ring in memory of a lost spouse?

Eight people gathered in the room, no one that she had met. Wasn't that why she had joined this group, because single parents tended to fade into the background?

"My name is Ted Edwards. And, folks, this is Verity Clark. She's a newcomer to our fellowship. Why don't you tell us a little about yourself—what brought you to this group, Verity."

Verity froze for a second, but of course they would want to know. "As Ted said, I'm Verity Clark. I've been working from home until recently."

A couple of people nodded, as if they did the same thing.

"But that job ended unexpectedly when the doctor's office closed. Only yesterday I started substituting at the high school. My husband was a marine who died five years ago."

Sympathetic murmurs greeted that statement.

"I have three children. Keenan's a high school sophomore, Des's in middle school and Mason's in second grade."

"You're Amity Finch's sister, aren't you? I went to school with her."

"Yes, I am." Amity was nine years younger than Verity. As the parents introduced themselves, Verity realized she was the oldest in the group and most of the members were more Amity's age. A couple of parents had children in middle school, but no older teens.

Different circumstances led them to their single state. The leader was a widower. Others were divorced, deserted, never married. There was even one mother whose husband was incarcerated.

The group had just started studying a book that would last for the next thirteen weeks of meetings. Verity paid for her copy, fifteen dollars she'd planned on saving toward new shoes for Keenan, and flipped through the pages. It seemed like a survival guide for newly single parents. Some of the questions she had asked and answered years ago. Others, such as dating, resonated with her current situation with Garrett. How could she talk about him with people who knew him? Maybe this was a mistake.

For all of her reservations, tonight's topic, "You're More than a Survivor," hit the mark for Verity. Survivor? Yes. More? Most days she felt like she was barely treading water.

When the younger parents talked about sleepless nights with sick children, Verity talked about the homework watch and staying awake until her children were in bed. When they talked about using their sick days for their children, she remembered the stacks of work she left unfinished when anything came up with her kids. Maybe the age of the children didn't matter as much as she thought it would.

Most of all, throughout the night, she wondered what Garrett would say. His advice made more sense than a lot of what she was hearing.

Garrett stayed behind in the Sunday school room for a few minutes after the youth spilled out, changing the posters for the next series of lessons. Someone shuffled in, and Garrett looked up.

"Garrett?" Keenan took a step into the room.

"Come on in and take a load off." Garrett sat on the couch, and Keenan sank into the comfy chair across from him.

"You like my mom."

Garrett opened his mouth, but Keenan spoke again. "Don't deny it. I know you do. And she's happier since you've been around. Even when she's mad at me for screwing up."

Garrett's eyebrows grew higher and higher with each word. He blinked. "Yes, I do care for Verity."

Keenan smirked, as if he had uncovered a secret weakness, so his next words surprised Garrett. "She doesn't like to leave us alone, and she's stopped asking me to keep an eye on things."

His resentment at being the live-in babysitter had come through clearly, and Verity had changed her behavior. Where was Keenan headed?

"But I want to take care of the kid so you two can go on a real date. On a Friday night, maybe, so Mom won't worry about school the next day."

Garrett couldn't stop a smile from spreading across his face. "Thanks, Keenan. I'll ask her." But what about Des?

Verity accepted the invitation, even after Garrett mentioned Des's reaction on New Year's Eve. On Friday night, moonlight danced across the white fields, icicles sparkling on the trees. It was a beautiful night for a second date.

Keenan opened the door to Garrett's knock. "Mom's getting ready."

She came out a few minutes later wearing a sweater and slacks, her hair brushed in a carefree style and diamond earrings adding to her elegant good looks. "Sorry I'm late," she said.

He didn't see Des before they left. Once they settled in the car, Garrett asked after her.

"She's at a friend's house, getting an early start on a project due later this month."

Verity's neutral tone sounded unnatural. Des's absence probably had more to do with his arrival than the school project.

"So where are we going?" Verity undid her coat as the heater warmed the car. "I didn't eat supper with the kids."

Garrett grinned. "We're headed to a place up in Stowe. It's a small place I discovered the last time I went skiing."

"Sounds wonderful." She looked at him sideways, a shy smile playing around her lips. "I still can't believe this was Keenan's idea."

He laughed. "A pleasant surprise. But..." He glanced at her.

"What?"

"I don't want to talk about kids tonight. Tonight is about you and me, two people who happened to meet."

That made her laugh. "We've known each other all our lives."

A stop sign loomed, and he took a moment to stare at her. "Not like this. Never like this."

"So what do you want to know about me?"

"A purely selfish question. What is the earliest memory you have of me?"

They kept to worry-free conversation, reliving joint memories from their childhoods, winking through small towns and past dark trees, guardians of the road, the moon filling the sky. They arrived in Stowe, where a tall white steeple dominated the skyline, with bridges and buildings that graced the front of many Christmas cards.

Thanks to Garrett's reservation, they were led straight to a table near the lively fireplace, where they could enjoy its warmth and see everything going on in the room.

Verity tucked her napkin in her lap and looked around. "This place is beautiful. And look at this menu, one page of perfect dishes. Even Travis couldn't find anything to complain about." Her brother-in-law, who, until he married Felicity, had helped resurrect failing bed-and-breakfasts though his reality TV show.

Garrett laughed. "I haven't thought of it that way, but I suppose so. I like it because the food is good."

"What do you recommend?" Verity peered at him over the top of the menu. "Everything sounds delicious."

Verity chose Garrett's recommendation. Dinner stretched out as they ate at a leisurely pace.

The conversation took a serious turn from their earlier banter. "What made you decide to become a truant officer? How old were you? It seems like an unusual occupation to choose," Verity said.

"One step above the tax collectors?" Garrett smiled.

"Definitely." Verity chuckled but waited for his answer.

"I started in prelaw, very ambitious, until I became a big brother. That made my thoughts turn to family law, child protection, maybe a guardian *ad litem*. The more involved I became with the kids, the more I thought being a truant officer could make a difference before things escalated far enough to need a lawyer." He finished his cup of coffee and signaled for another. He'd pay for the caffeine in the morning, but he enjoyed their brew. He settled back in his chair with a satisfied sigh. "I thought I could escape the courtroom—and the suits—but that's a big part of my job now. I go to court at least once a month, usually more like three or four times."

Verity finished about half of her sixteen-ounce steak before she pushed it away. "Will you be embarrassed if I ask for a doggie bag?"

"As long as you save room to share dessert with me."

Verity laughed again. Her head tilted back, her eyes scrunched, showing tiny lines at their corners, her cheeks a pretty pink. He decided to make her laugh as much as possible.

For dessert, the server brought a hot fudge sundae. They had just dipped their spoons into the ice cream when Verity's phone rang.

"It's Keenan," she said before she answered. "What's happened?" All the laughter had left her face. She listened to his explanation. "I'll be right there."

Garrett froze, readying himself for bad news.

"Des never came home from her friend's house."

Chapter 12

Verity wanted to chew the nails she had painted so carefully that afternoon. She thanked God that Garrett was driving, so that she could make phone calls and learn something—anything—before they arrived in Maple Notch.

Des didn't answer her cell, and neither did her friend, NancyJo Andrews. What mischief had the longtime friends gotten into? Verity gave Garrett a running commentary in between calls.

After five minutes of frantic calling, Verity reached Mrs. Andrews. "This is Verity Clark, Des's mother. Is she with NancyJo?"

"Des?" Mrs. Andrews sounded surprised. "Not today. NancyJo isn't home tonight, either. She's out with friends."

"Would you please check? Maybe she slipped in." Her request sounded silly even to herself, but Mrs. Andrews agreed.

A minute later, she picked the phone up again. "Neither one of them is here. I'll call you when I learn something."

"Me, too." Verity's fears doubled.

"What did she say?" Garrett asked.

"Des hasn't been there all week. And tonight, NancyJo isn't home, either."

Garrett glanced at the dashboard clock. "It's ten o'clock on a Friday night. Maybe they're out with friends."

His neutral tone didn't fool Verity. "She's just thirteen. If—and I do mean if—I had agreed to her staying out so late, I'd know exactly where she was going." Her shoulders shook. "First Keenan, and now this? I must be a terrible mother."

Garrett didn't respond, not even with the knee-jerk statement, "Of course not." He rubbed his chin, eyes flickering as thoughts raced through his mind.

"What do you think might have happened? What should I do?" She wanted answers.

Garrett blew out his breath. "We'll go to your apartment first. Call all of Des's friends that you know. I've got the numbers of kids in the church youth group, if you need them."

Verity nodded as another friend picked up. "Hello, Lilli. It's Des's mom, Mrs. Clark. Have you seen Des or NancyJo tonight?...No? Thanks for your time." By the time they reached the outskirts of Maple Notch, Verity had exhausted the contact numbers on her phone.

Garrett said, "After I drop you off, I'll go to the church for the kids' addresses."

"Stay with me." The words came out dry and scratchy.

A smile crossed Garrett's face as if her request pleased him and he nodded. "I'll stop by the church first, then, to pick up the roster."

The silence in the car roared in Verity's mind. Her

throat choked, making her incapable of speech. Tears blinded her.

She clung to Garrett's steady breathing, in and out, in and out, while she wrung the handkerchief she'd had the foresight to carry with her.

At the church parking lot, Garrett set his hand on the door handle. "God heard all those prayers."

"What prayers?" She hadn't even cried to God for help.

"Your tears. You know, the prayers that can't be uttered?"

She hiccuped and nodded.

"Do you want to come in with me?" he asked.

She shook her head. While he was gone, she prayed for protection for both girls, wherever they were. For success in finding them. Asking God to take over since she was such a failure. First Keenan, now Des.

A few minutes later, Garrett returned and handed her the list. "I added a couple of kids who've visited recently."

Verity scanned the names and she remembered something Des had said recently. "I can't ask anyone over here. They all have nice houses."

"You can't blame yourself," Garrett said quietly.

Verity jumped, then shook her head. "Keenan felt neglected because of Mason. I should have known Des was under pressure, too."

They had arrived at the apartment. "Just remember one thing. God loves Des more than you do."

True, but tell that to the parents who lost children to drunk drivers or drugs. Verity leaned on Garrett's arm as they mounted the stairs, feeling as rubbery as a wet noodle.

Keenan was on the phone when they walked in. Mason wasn't in sight, nor Des, though Verity had secretly hoped she would be home. Verity tiptoed to the boys' room, her heartbeat roaring in her ears. Mason lay blissfully asleep, and she released the breath she didn't know she had been holding.

"Mom," Keenan said. Mason wiggled, then flopped to his other side.

She slid from his room and down the hall. "What is it?"

The serious expression on Garrett's face scared her. "We think we know where Des is."

Verity flopped on the sofa as adrenaline drained from her body.

"Verity." Garrett's voice cut through the fog clouding her brain. Something was wrong, something they didn't want to tell her. Her knees jerked nervously.

"There was a big party tonight, at Brad's house," Keenan said.

The name sounded vaguely familiar.

"He's a football jock, and so are most of his friends. But his sister is Des's age. I think Des might be there."

"Where is it?" Possibilities swam through Verity's mind. Older teens could mean drugs, alcohol, sex…

"I don't know Brad myself," Garrett said. "And I haven't heard anything about him, except what I've read in the newspaper articles about the games." He grinned, although his eyes didn't agree. "In my line of business, that's a good thing."

Verity closed her eyes. *God's in control.* "Let's go. Keenan, do you mind…"

Her son already had his jacket on. "I want to come with you. I can get in easier than you."

Verity looked to Garrett. Oh, how she wished he could come with her.

Instead, he said, "I'll stay here with Mason. Go on ahead."

* * *

Garrett paced back and forth on the living room carpet, praying. Why did he have to stay behind while Verity fought this latest battle?

Because Verity was Des's mother, that's why.

Finally keys in the lock alerted him to their return. The door opened and Keenan entered first.

"Go ahead." Verity, still out of sight, voice tired and terse.

Des schlepped in, hoodie hiding her face, shoulders slumped. She came within two feet of Garrett's shoes and stopped. "You." She came toe-to-toe with him. "I'm sorry I was so rude to you."

The mumbled words had no commitment behind them, but she had made an effort. "It's okay, Des. You must know I mean you no harm."

Des harrumphed before she hung up her coat by the door. Verity came in, her appearance sending waves of pain through Garrett. She was so worried, hurt, determined. Stronger than he had expected. "Thank you for staying with Mason. We can catch up later."

"I'm glad you're safe, Des." Garrett stood at the door. "I'm sorry," he said to Verity, helplessly.

She shook her head and mouthed, "Later."

Heavyhearted, Garrett headed for his house. When he arrived at the crossroads, he turned to the left. Even though it was almost eleven at night, Aunt Hazel might be up. Ever since Keenan had shoveled her driveway, she had asked after the family.

Her porch light came on as soon as his car pulled into the driveway. She opened the door for him. "Come on in. I've got the makings for hot cocoa in the kitchen."

"How did you know to expect me?" Garrett followed her into the familiar kitchen, cheerful with daisy-printed curtains. Many happy childhood memories centered around the maple table.

"Keenan called while he was waiting to get back. If you hadn't come by soon, I was going to call you."

Keenan had called Aunt Hazel?

"Keenan has stopped by several times since he shoveled my driveway. I think he's adopted me as a grandmother, since his father's mother is out of state, and of course, Verity's mother died a while back." Aunt Hazel added a dollop of whipped cream to the cocoa and handed him the mug.

"You always did pick up strays." Garrett sat back in the chair. "You listened to my adolescent angst, and gave me pointers when I needed them."

Aunt Hazel laughed. "Or a good kick in the pants."

"So what has it been for Keenan, advice or warning?" Garrett sipped the cocoa. "You're not a psychiatrist. Can't claim confidentiality."

"And you're not a cop."

Garrett lifted his eyebrows. "I am a friend."

"So far, I haven't had opportunity to say much of anything. He comes over, showing off those new muscles while he helps around the house."

Garrett stayed quiet, letting his aunt's brand of cocoa and counsel give a balm to his soul. When he finished the cocoa, his aunt served him a chaser of chamomile tea and honey. "He hasn't said much, but it's clear he thinks a lot of you. And that he's glad you're dating his mother." Her eyes twinkled, as if she had discovered his deep secret.

He didn't dispute her. "Keenan isn't the problem, though. Des, his sister, has made it clear she doesn't like me. She went to a party tonight, with older kids, and didn't let Verity know."

"Did Verity blame you?"

"Not in so many words." Garrett shrugged.

"Oh, my." Aunt Hazel put the cups in the dishwasher and laid a hand on his shoulder. "I got your old room ready. Sleep if you can."

Garrett accepted the offer. The closet held an assortment of his clothes, just as a parent's house would. Tomorrow he would change his date duds for jeans and T-shirt. He glanced at the clock. Make that later this morning.

He dressed for bed and lay there, staring at the sparkling stars on the ceiling. He and Nick had placed them there as boys. Now as then, his thoughts turned to God when he studied the sky. "The heavens declare the glory of God; the skies proclaim the work of His hands." God's greatness brought enough peace for Garrett to fall asleep.

The next morning, Keenan showed up about the time Garrett was eating breakfast. "Good morning, Keenan. I want you to take me shopping for tomorrow's dinner." Aunt Hazel winked at Garrett. "I've invited the Clarks to eat with me, to thank them for Keenan's help."

Keenan grinned, the most carefree Garrett had ever seen him. He grabbed a doughnut, munching with the hollow-leg appetite of a teenage boy. Garrett couldn't afford to indulge his appetite like that anymore, not if he wanted to keep his football physique.

Face it. He wanted to look good for Verity. The thought brought him crashing down to reality. "How's your…? What happened—after I left last night?"

Keenan finished the doughnut as he sat down. After he washed it down with a glass of milk, he said, "Des said all kinds of crazy things. I've been mad at Mom, too, but I never treated her like that."

No, he had quietly rebelled, but he was making up for his mistakes. Garrett had no right to ask how Verity was doing. The question he should ask stalled on his tongue, almost choking him. He swallowed a mouthful of coffee. "Is it me?"

Aunt Hazel nodded her support.

"She doesn't know what she's talking about," Keenan said.

So Des did blame him. Sadness settled over Garrett like a cold winter fog.

"You're good for Mom." Keenan took a bite of another doughnut. "Don't give up. Stick around, no matter what Des says."

Two sleepless nights followed Friday's debacle. Whenever Verity did slip into sleep, Des flopped over on the top bunk and woke her up. Instead of praying about Des, Verity found herself reliving her date with Garrett. When she woke early Sunday morning, she gave up on sleep and got out of bed.

Sundays filled Verity with hope for a new start. She usually felt refreshed and renewed after worship, but not today. After Des's behavior on Friday, Verity didn't care to put her in Garrett's class. If they went to their old church, they'd be peppered with questions and concern.

Verity needed to talk with a friend, one who was always up at this hour. She left a note on the kitchen table—"Gone to the tea shop"—and headed out.

As her car trundled over the concrete-and-steel bridge, she imagined crossing on a covered bridge, in a simpler time. She arrived at the tea shop five minutes later. Felicity was her normal perky self, her face and apron dotted with color and flour.

"So what are you throwing together?" Verity asked. The Sunday menu featured the muffin and cupcake of the week.

"White on white. Winter in Vermont at its best," Felicity said.

"But with a twist, I'm sure. You're not putting seven-minute frosting on vanilla cake." Verity looked across the table.

"Of course not." Felicity touched her sister on the nose. "What do you smell?" Felicity loved this game, which she always won.

Verity spied a tray of cupcakes on the counter and took a bite. "Angel food."

"You cheated." Felicity shook her finger at her sister. "With a hint of white grape juice and cucumber. In the filling, I've got green grapes, hazelnuts and coconut."

Verity took a second bite and sighed with complete satisfaction. She could eat the entire tray, slip into a sugar-induced nap and forget about everything for a while. Instead, she began chopping hazelnuts.

They worked side by side for a few minutes without speaking. The timer dinged and Felicity slid one pan of cupcakes out, a tray of muffins taking its place. "So when are you going to tell me why you're over here at the crack of dawn?" Felicity asked.

Verity closed her eyes. "I don't know where to start."

"At the beginning? Do-re-me and all that?" As girls, they had watched the *The Sound of Music* over and over again after they visited the Von Trapp Family Lodge in Stowe.

"My favorite things." Verity recovered a short, happy moment. "I remember saying your muffins and the first day of spring were two of my favorite things." She fell silent again.

"The beginning?" Felicity prompted.

"I'm thinking about skipping church." Verity jumped to the end.

Dumbfounded, Felicity stopped chopping. "That's not like you, but you wouldn't drive over here to tell me that.

You haven't even told us you changed churches. Nick had to tell us."

"Sorry." Verity took another sip of coffee and chopped more hazelnuts.

"Is it Keenan?" Felicity stirred the chopped ingredients together.

"No, he's fine. He even offered to watch Mason so I could go on a date with Garrett." Verity avoided her sister's eyes, afraid of what she might see there.

Felicity laughed. "I knew it! I couldn't be happier." She stirred the ingredients a moment before stopping again. "So what's the problem? He's one of the good guys."

Verity moaned. "Remember when you used to come to me for dating advice?"

"Ayuh." The timer dinged, and Felicity pulled the last muffins from the oven. "Want to help me with breakfast prep?"

Verity spilled the whole story while she chopped the vegetables needed for the morning's menu.

Felicity said, "So now Keenan is doing better, and he likes Garrett, but Des is acting out."

"Welcome to my world." Verity swept the veggies into containers and pulled plastic wrap over them. "And now I'd better get home."

"Come to the Community Church this morning. We're your family. No one will question you, just give you some TLC."

Verity weighed her options as she drove home. Mason was watching cartoons, a trail of wet cereal rings following him from kitchen to carpet. "Good morning, sport."

He blinked, as if surprised to see her standing there. "Hi. I got cereal." He lifted his bowl, sloshing a little more on the floor.

"So I see." She sat on the couch next to him. "What

would you think of going to Grandpa's church this morning?"

"Sure." The TV commercials ended and Mason riveted his attention on the screen again.

Verity climbed in the shower. The steamy heat eased her sore muscles and relieved her short breaths. She got out and wrapped an old robe around herself, one Curtis had given her.

The clock told her they needed to get moving to make it to church in time. She turned on the light in Keenan's room. "Rise and shine."

He groaned but rolled out of bed.

In the girls' room, Des was already up. "Where have you been?"

"I left a note on the kitchen table." Verity's voice trailed off.

"I freaked. Your bed was empty and your coat was gone. You were so mad at me for going to the party."

"You lied," Verity said.

"But you disappeared this morning." Des turned her back on her mother, and grabbed a pair of jeans. "Where did you go?"

Verity badly wanted to say "none of your business" but bit off the answer that rose to her lips. "I went to see your aunt Felicity. I talked with her about you and Keenan and…Garrett."

Chapter 13

Garrett couldn't keep still on Sunday morning, looking over the shoulders of every kid as he arrived as if Keenan and Des would magically appear. When they didn't arrive before opening prayer, he dragged his attention away from the door to the class. The Clarks weren't coming.

After the group broke up, Keenan came in, without Des. Her absence hurt, her mother's hurt more. After class, Keenan approached Garrett. "I asked Aaron for a ride. Mom's gone to our old church."

Garrett struggled to keep his composure. "Did Des and Mason go with her?" His voice squeaked.

"Yes." Keenan looked away, as if embarrassed.

Come on, Garrett, you're the adult here. He cleared his throat. "That's good. They're worshipping the Lord. As the Bible says, one faith, one Lord, one baptism."

"Des hates the old church. But…"

The classroom had emptied. "Do you want to stay and hang for a few?" Garrett asked.

Keenan's shrug didn't answer, but he dropped onto the floppy couch the teens seemed to love.

Garrett decided to open the discussion. "Des may not want to come to a class that I'm teaching. And a visit with old friends will help your mom." If a visit was all it was. He didn't envy the decisions facing Verity, and dreaded the way they might affect him. The last thing either one of them wanted was for the girl to refuse to go to church at all.

Keenan scoffed. "There's mostly old people at the church. They're nice, but it's like going to a family reunion."

"Is that so bad?" Keenan's comment reminded Garrett of an upcoming event. "Speaking of family reunions, we're having our midwinter weekend in the Reid Cave next month. Are you interested?"

Keenan chuckled. "Aunt Amity talks about it all the time. She says members of the Reid and Tuttle families from all around the country participate during the summer. But the winter trip is the best for locals. She calls us the 'pure bloods,' since we never escaped Maple Notch." He looked at Garrett. "Yeah, I'd like to go. But I have a question for you. What made you decide to stay in this small town? People say you were good enough to play in the NFL."

That conversation with Keenan came back to Garrett's mind when he met Verity for lunch on Thursday. Felicity had recommended a Mexican restaurant in Churchbridge, her husband's hometown.

"I feel like I'm sixteen again, sneaking away when my parents won't know I'm gone." Verity patted her pocket. "I've got my phone with me, in case anyone tries to call."

Garrett's lips curled in a smile. He wanted to cut the umbilical cord. "That's part of the reason why I wanted to talk with you today."

"What? To tell me I shouldn't let my thirteen-year-old daughter dictate how I live my life?" Verity bit into a tortilla chip, and the crunch filled the silence. "I know that. I love my kids, I really do, but I want a life apart from my children."

Garrett didn't answer the rhetorical question. "Is the single-parents group any help?"

She shook her head. "Not really. They try different things. Some of them swap babysitting, so that they can have nights out. Some of them have families who help out." She chuckled, and spicy dip dribbled from the corner of her mouth. She grabbed her napkin. "And a couple of them share custody with their exes. They talk about how lonely it is when their children aren't there."

"And you wish you could have some time alone." Garrett understood. "Do any of them have teens? Besides my sister?"

Verity shook her head. "A few have kids in elementary school. One of the boys is in Mason's class. They all heard about Mason last year, when he was so sick. And your sister hasn't been there when I've been there." She pushed the bowl of chips away from her. "I'm not that hungry. Do you mind going for a walk?"

They left the restaurant a few minutes later, after Garrett arranged for takeout when they finished their walk. A few patches of ice remained on the sidewalks, and tall piles of snow lined the streets. Verity unzipped her hoodie and let it fall on her back. "Nothing like brisk winter air to clear my senses."

Garrett reached for her hand. He would gladly delay his lunch for a few minutes alone with Verity.

They came to a corner and Verity pointed to the right. "Felicity's father-in-law lives around here." They walked down the street dotted with houses a lot like the ones in

Maple Notch, although none matched the elegance of the Bailey mansion.

"On Sunday, Keenan asked me about playing in the NFL."

"Oh, that." Pink played across Verity's face. "I've told him a bit about your more famous moments. How you were drafted by the Giants when you were in college."

Garrett groaned. "I don't talk about it much. It wasn't my best moment."

"Nonsense." Verity stopped and took his hands in hers. "You were on your way to playing professional football when you had that accident. Instead of letting it destroy you, you decided to help kids instead."

"The accident got my attention, to head me down the road God had planned for me all along."

Verity let go of his hand and drew close, raising her head as if inviting him to kiss her ruby-red lips. He brushed her lips, her breath slightly spicy, but nonetheless sweet. A kiss of a moment could change a lifetime. He lifted his lips but kept his head bent over hers. "What are we going to do, Verity?"

Verity stepped away, knowing the kiss was a mistake. Shaking her head, she took another step away. "I don't know. I can't keep doing this." Her voice wobbled, betraying her inner turmoil. "I'm not a twenty-two-year-old coed looking for the man I want to spend the rest of my life with. Instead, I'm a thirty-eight-year-old single mother responsible for raising the children God has given me." Her voice shook. "And God forgive me if I want more."

Flames leaped in Garrett's eyes. He stiffened, starting at his shoulders, down his chest and legs until his feet looked like they were riveted to the molten rock. "I've always thought you weren't ready for a serious relationship, but I hoped I was wrong."

Stung by the icy edge to his words, Verity asked, "How? What?"

He took her hand, not the gentle sharing of a moment ago, but more like grasping a tool. He stripped her glove from her right hand, and tapped her ring finger. "That's what told me. Curtis may have gone to heaven five years ago, but he still lives at the center of your heart, right next to those three children." He released her hands until only their fingernails touched. "And God help me, that's one of the reasons why I'm growing to love you."

Bewildered, flummoxed, Verity didn't speak as they walked back to the restaurant parking lot. Only three inches separated them, but they might as well have been on opposite sides of the Atlantic.

They reached the back of the restaurant before Garrett paused. "I'll know you're ready to move forward without reservation when you take that ring off. Until then, I'll keep our contacts to a minimum." He chuckled ruefully. "And pray that Keenan keeps on the straight and narrow."

Stung by Garrett's conclusion, Verity picked up her pace, going directly to her car. Garrett hurried to catch up, but she ignored him until she reached her car. Turning to him, she said, "If I can convince Des we're not dating, maybe she'll be willing to come back to church." Blinking back the tears that wanted to escape, she opened the door.

Garrett put his hand on the door. "Wait a minute. Please. I ordered dinner to go."

Acid rose in her throat. "I told you. I'm not hungry."

Garrett pulled back reluctantly, and she edged her car out of the parking spot. On the road home, she attempted to forget the past hour, to notice the road and only the road, to drive safely without distractions. Along the way, she saw a doe peeking through trees, and a moose bugled in the distance. As she drove under the bare-limbed trees, a flock of birds flew away. A single feather landed on her windshield.

The God who knew every time a sparrow fell must also know when one lost a feather. Stopping by the side of the road, she removed the feather from the car and ran her finger along the soft edge, holding it next to her cheek. Looking at the sky, she said, "Thank You, Lord. I needed that reminder today."

Back home, she checked her phone for messages. Her position as the replacement English teacher was confirmed. Even though she had asked for the opportunity, had prayed about it and thanked God for it, she couldn't shake the numbness in her heart.

She looked at her wedding ring, twisting it around her finger, remembering the day she and Curtis vowed to love each other until death. Death had severed them, her vow fulfilled. No, Curtis hadn't fulfilled the vow. He had died and left her alone, dreams unfilled, with three children to raise on her own.

She stretched out on the sofa and hugged the sofa cushion, crying. The door rattled, startling Verity awake. It was 2:45—Des must be home. Verity dashed into the bathroom and wiped her face with a damp washcloth, erasing the evidence of tears. When Des came in, she hugged her daughter close. "I love you."

Des managed a muffled, "I love you, too," before she pushed away. In the kitchen, Verity looked for something to offer Des as a snack, then shook her head. The days when a peanut butter cookie could solve a child's problems were long gone. Then again, eating offered a chance for conversation. Rethinking, she reached for a couple of apples, washed them, before polishing their shine set to appeal.

Des accepted the apple without comment or a thank-you, but Verity had greater concerns. She sat down, and plumped the cushion next to her. "How are you?"

"Ugh. Homework." Des scrunched her face. "I have to read a hundred more pages and write a book report before tomorrow morning." Backpack in hand, she headed for the bedroom.

The prayer Verity sent heavenward didn't seem to get past the ceiling. She picked up the women's magazine she had purchased because it featured an article titled "How to Build a Business on the Internet" on the cover. Reading, it sounded as though anyone with a computer and time had all the resources they needed to make it rich. Resting her head against the cushion, she scanned the article. Ten ways to start a successful business in one page. She'd rather teach, but she'd have to get her certificate first before she could get a permanent job.

Valentine's Day came and went, and once again Garrett had no one to celebrate with. Every time he walked past the room where Verity was teaching English literature to high school freshmen, he wanted to wave. Instead, he satisfied himself with an occasional shared glance.

Des had calmed down enough to come back to Sunday school. This weekend, he would spend time with the younger members of his extended family, including Keenan.

When Garrett had offered to pick up Keenan, Verity had agreed. Hopefully Des wouldn't take that as dating, even if they chatted for a few minutes. No such luck—as soon as he knocked, Keenan opened the door. His backpack was filled with all the extras the twenty-first century offered campers in the wild.

"We'll be back Sunday afternoon," Garrett said, waving to the family in general, while Keenan rattled down the steps to the car.

A few minutes later, they were on the road, Keenan buckled in after a reminder from Garrett. "I should have made you walk to the cave. After all, that was how they had to travel during the Revolutionary War. Or a horse, of course."

"Then you should walk, too," Keenan quipped.

Garrett took the long route to the cave. He turned onto the main road heading toward the Tuttle Bridge, and stopped by a historical marker that most passersby ignored.

"Have you ever read the marker?" Garrett asked.

Keenan scratched his head. "I don't think so."

"Then your lessons this weekend begin now." Garrett parked at the side of the road. Up close, the words were as faded and difficult to read as many others of their kind across the country. Nevertheless, he could recite the description word for word, closing his eyes to imagine the empty field that occupied the space during the Revolutionary War. He summarized. "We are going to a cave where a new widow stayed with her four children during the war. They slept by day and farmed by night, in the field where a house now stood, because the Tories in Maple Notch had taken over all the farms. Their courage, and helped by the son of a Tory father, helped Maple Notch get rid of the Tories for the duration of the war."

"And we're their great-great-somethings. Sally Reid and Josiah Tuttle." Keenan shrugged. "Aunt Amity's been telling me the stories of the first settlers in this area."

A cold wind blew down the road and the two of them

dug deeper into their coats, heading back to the warm car. Where had the courage of their ancestors gone?

"You promise the cave will be warm?"

"Warm? Maybe not." Garrett chuckled. "You may not be comfortable, but I promise you won't get sick."

Only four boys were coming this year, including Keenan and his friend Aaron Reid. Amity would bring girls the following month. What Garrett lacked in her storytelling skills, he made up for in re-creating life in the eighteenth century.

The original covered bridge that crossed the Bumblebee River was located near the cave. To reach it from the modern bridge, they pulled off the road in a small parking area. A steep, winding staircase led from the overhang to the cave opening.

The other parents had just dropped off their sons. Aaron set his foot on the first step when Garrett spoke up. "Hold on. Join me over here." He stood at a spot that terrified most of the girls, or anyone with a fear of heights, because they looked straight into the river, high, deep and swift at this time of year. "Be thankful you don't have to scramble down that bank without the benefit of the stairs, like the first Reids did. Mrs. Reid did it every night, even when she was eight months pregnant. So I don't want to hear any complaints this weekend."

A few grumblings made Garrett smile. This weekend could be life-changing. "The stairs may look old and rickety, but they're safe enough." Garrett went down first to demonstrate, waiting at the bottom as the boys spilled onto the thin strip of land between the cave and the river. "Watch out for your heads." Again, he led the way, stooping at his waist to avoid hitting his head.

Keenan didn't stoop low enough and bumped his head.

"They must have been short back then, to walk around in here."

"Most of them were," Garrett said.

Aaron came in, blocking the sunlight from coming through. "Who turned off the light?"

Light laughter followed, their uncertainty palpable.

"First step tonight—get a fire going."

The boys looked at one another uneasily. "We don't have to chop down a tree, do we?" Keenan asked.

"No. But you do have to find kindling for the fire."

Aaron asked, "Can we look that up on our phones?"

Garrett said, "Ayuh. Just don't order it online."

More laughter followed.

"Tonight, we'll make pointed sticks and roast hot dogs over the fire. Tomorrow we're going to hunt for food on our own."

They ate every hot dog Garrett brought with them, while he outlined the agenda for Saturday. The boys settled into their bedrolls and chattered late into the night. By tomorrow night, they would fall asleep as soon as their heads hit their pillows.

Garrett lay on his old blanket, considering the obstacles his ancestors had overcome. Mrs. Reid was a widow, like Verity, when she lived in the cave. If she could survive and thrive for thirty more years, there must be hope for their future.

Soon, though, Lord. Please make it soon. Garrett went to sleep.

Chapter 14

When Keenan returned from his weekend cave camp late Sunday afternoon, Garrett waved hello but didn't come in. Keenan didn't stop talking about the weekend until late that night. He hadn't talked so much since the last time he slept outside, on a church retreat a couple of years ago.

"Maybe we should go camping this summer." Verity laid the bait before the children.

"Yeah!" Mason jumped in the air.

"And I know how to start a fire." Keenan's chest puffed out.

"Ugh," Des said. "Snakes and black flies and dirt."

Verity tilted her head. "You're invited to the girls' campout next month. Don't you want to go?"

"Aunt Amity leads it up. She knows lots of stuff, interesting stuff," Keenan said. His enthusiasm pleased her. "Garrett says she's really good.

"Will you stop talking about Garrett this and Garrett

that, as if he's the only man who knows anything about all those dead people or how to start a fire." Des pulled her sweater tight around her. "It's too cold to go camping in March. I don't see how you stood it."

"Don't be stupid. Garrett won't be at the cave during the girls' weekend."

Des stomped her foot. "Mom. Keenan's bossing me around."

Verity shut her eyes. "It's her decision, Keenan. I think you'd have fun, Des, but you don't have to go." She'd hate for her daughter to miss the experience because she was mad at Garrett.

When March rolled around, Des didn't change her mind. The room she shared with Verity felt smaller with every passing day. The days they both suffered from PMS were miserable, and Verity couldn't blame it all on Des. Mason ran around the house, all pent-up energy while waiting for spring to arrive, and neighbors complained about the noise.

Most of all, she missed spending time with Garrett. That was also the good news. After several weeks of waving long distance, they had started sharing lunch. On Friday, she headed for the teachers' lounge to eat and unwind. After she consumed her sack lunch, she leaned back, closing her eyes.

"Hey there."

At the sound of the familiar voice, a smile flashed across Verity's face and she opened her eyes. "I was hoping you'd stop by."

"Come on." He grabbed her hand. "It's a beautiful spring day, and you should have just enough time—" he looked at his watch "—to go for a quick ride before your next class."

Verity giggled as he led her down a back stairwell to

the employee parking lot. "Someone will see us." Des? The middle school didn't face this way. "Am I allowed to leave campus during the day?"

"As long as you're back in your classroom at 11:42, ready to teach the wonders of *David Copperfield*, you'll be fine."

A few, carefree minutes with the best man in the world was a treat too good to resist. They jumped in Garrett's car and headed down the road. "Oh, look at that."

"What is it?" Garrett glanced before he turned his attention back to the road.

"Buds on the pine trees. Those little bits of spring green."

"Let's have a look." Garrett pulled over. They danced through the trees, and Garrett threw a pinecone at her.

Verity threw it back. The game of catch with pointed cones continued until one landed on the shirt pocket with a decided rip. A glance at her watch told her she only had five minutes until class began. She couldn't return dressed as she was.

At the car, Garrett tossed something to her, a sweatshirt from the high school, in faded green and gold.

Garrett floored the pedal, driving at least ten miles over the speed limit.

"Slow down. Getting a speeding ticket won't help." She looked at the sweatshirt. "I shouldn't wear this."

"Why not? There's a spirit rally at the school this afternoon, and a big home game tonight. Didn't you see everybody in their school colors?"

"That's true. Thank you." The sleeves hung over her hands, even when she rolled them up. It hung low enough to pass for a dress. "No one will believe this is mine."

"Maybe they'll think it's from your high school flame." Garrett wiggled his eyebrows, making her laugh.

He dropped her by the front entrance as the class bell rang. By running up the steps and down the hall, she made it to her class as the final bell rang. She stopped, took a deep breath and walked in.

When she reached her desk, she realized she had forgotten something. Her briefcase, with her teaching materials, sat on the floor of Garrett's car.

Garrett drove halfway to his office before he noticed Verity's briefcase. She clung to it like a lifeline, pulling out the material at odd moments to study and review. What a great excuse to see her again. With a grin, he turned the car around and headed back to the high school.

Whistling, he parked in the employee lot and raced up the steps. He paused in front of the water fountain for a drink just as Des came out of the girls' bathroom. "Mr. Sawtelle."

Her voice wavered between a whimper and fingernails on chalkboard. "Des. Good to see you."

Ignoring his greeting, she pointed to the briefcase. "What are you doing with Mom's briefcase?"

Simplest was best. "I'm returning it to her."

Des didn't budge, her books piled on one arm, her other arm angled to her hip. "How come you have it?" Her voice remained quiet, as if she didn't want anyone to hear her. "Did you...?"

"Yes, we spent lunch together." Garrett matched Des's near-whisper. "I've got to get this to your mom, so she has her lesson plans." He started to walk away but turned back. "And if you're angry with anybody, be mad at me, not your mother. Now get to class. You're late."

Her face twisted in a frown and she whirled around, heading up the stairs. He jogged down the hall to the next flight of stairs and took the steps two at a time, to reach the top floor where most of the English classes were held. His watch told him the class was half-over when he reached the door. A peek through the window relieved his worries. Verity sat on the teacher's desk, perfectly at ease, as if she wasn't wearing a sweatshirt that didn't belong to her. To his eyes, she looked good in it.

She was evidently improvising a lesson. The students in the first few rows—the only ones he could see—were raising their hands and smiling. With Verity's smile as confirmation, he'd guess the class was a great success. She made a great teacher—she should finish what she started and get her teaching certificate.

Since he didn't need to interrupt a successful lesson, he prowled the halls, checking on his clients. Five found, including Keenan, three missing. The office confirmed their absences, and he returned to Verity's room before the bell rang.

The students exited, the discussion from the class still raging. A couple of them waved and he returned the greeting. When the last kid left, Garrett entered, holding the briefcase in front of him. "I found this on the front seat."

"Thank God." Verity clapped her hands together. "I was so worried I had lost it. I barely made it through the past hour." She pulled a folder out and began sorting through the papers.

"You had that class in the palm of your hand," Garrett said. "You absolutely should be a teacher."

"You think so?" Verity's expression turned sad. "Only one problem. I don't have a teaching certificate."

"You can get one." Garrett slipped into mentor mode. "Get a loan, go back to school."

Verity looked exasperated, as if he had just suggested she take a shuttle to the moon. Two students came in. "I'm sorry, my next class is starting."

Garrett left before he remembered to tell her about Des. He sent a text, to alert her before school ended.

Verity didn't answer except to say she would talk with Des. The weekend crawled by, and Garrett itched for the school week to start again.

When Des showed up for Sunday school, Garrett was surprised. Sure, she avoided looking at him, but took part in singing and discussion. After class, Keenan handed him a paper bag with his sweatshirt inside. "Mom asked me to give this to you." He winked, and Garrett's face heated like a schoolboy. Inside the worship center, Mason waved, beckoning him over.

Garrett paused, uncertain whether to approach until Verity smiled and motioned for him to join her. With a bit of football swagger, he crossed the sanctuary to their pew. "Hello! It's good to have you back again."

Des didn't look at him, but she didn't make a face, either. Mason almost shook his hand off. And Verity—her timid smile made his heart weep. In spite of Verity's welcome, his presence made them uncomfortable.

"Thanks for returning the sweatshirt."

At Garrett's statement, Des wiggled a little.

"You're welcome." Verity pointed to the seat next to her. "I saved a space for you." Des wiggled again, but Verity didn't back down. Garrett was far more aware of Verity's arm brushing his than the sermon, and as soon as the service ended, the kids ran in different directions. Only Verity and Garrett lingered.

They headed toward the exit before speaking. He stood in front of her, sheltering her from the icy blasts every time someone opened the door. With his high school shirt tucked in the bag under his arm, he felt like he had gone back in time to his days as the star quarterback.

Dating was so much easier then, but now he was more

interested in finding "the one." And now that he felt as if he might have found her, every day he fought a battle to win her. *Lord, can you give me my Eve the way You did for Adam?*

He opened his eyes to Verity's wide, genuine smile. "I told Des we were coming here today and she didn't fuss about it. I think Keenan has been talking with her."

Garrett pulled her into a nook where the exiting crowd didn't file through. "I want to date you publicly. Keeping it a secret isn't working." The words came out without planning, but he wasn't sorry for what he had said.

"Like going steady?" Verity's own giggle sounded high-pitched to her, like a high school girl when the handsomest boy in her class asks her to the prom.

"Something like that." Garrett's face relaxed into a comfortable smile, one that showed the dimple in his chin. "I want to pick you up at your door next Friday night, for dinner and a movie. In front of all the children."

Verity hugged herself, her mouth widening as sunshine happiness glowed within. It dimmed as quickly as it arose. "I would say yes, but I can't go out this weekend." She hadn't planned to share the latest roadblock this way, but now she had to. "I didn't sign a new contract. Rent raised too high. We have to move by the end of the month." The news sucked more happiness out of her.

The door opened. "Mom?" Mason came in. "When are we going home?"

"Now." Verity looked at Garrett. "Maybe you can join us tonight? For planning and pizza?" *Give Des a test run*, but she didn't say it out loud.

Garrett nodded, and Mason cheered.

Lunch was a disjointed affair, the pot roast a little dry. Des didn't say much. Texts interrupted Keenan. If they kept up at this rate, she'd have to ban the phone from the table. Mason filled the silence with his chatter.

Before he could mention Garrett, Verity said, "Garrett is coming here tonight."

"Mom." Des's distress showed in the two-syllables she made of the word.

Reminding herself one last time she had reached the decision after much prayer, Verity said, "I invited him, Des. We don't want to hide anything from you."

After a glare that shouted her disappointment, Des buried her nose in her book before heading for her bunk. Aaron picked up Keenan to watch football at his house. Mason begged Verity to play a few board games before he got interested in a kids' show on TV.

Newspaper in hand, Verity settled in her favorite chair in the living room, the one Curtis loved to sit in. The chair was as dated as the way she had clung to widow weeds. Both the fashion and attitude needed to be updated. A wry grin shaped her mouth. At least changing her attitude didn't cost money.

She shook her head and turned to the want ads in the back. Most of the apartments were near the University of Vermont, in Burlington. She wanted to find a three-bedroom place, but the price would skyrocket.

She looked overhead, wishing she had a sky roof. *Lord, you take care of birds and flowers, and You'll take care of us. Is it asking too much, though, to ask for something better?*

Her prayer sparked a thought in her brain. At the top of a sheet of notepaper she wrote Things I Want in a House. Tapping the eraser end of her pencil on her chin, she first thought of all the things she didn't want. But she didn't want a wish list based on negatives. Half an hour later, her list looked like a pie-in-the-sky, miracle-necessary wish list.

She read through it again. Four bedrooms. At first she'd thought of three bedrooms, but Keenan needed a room of his own. A fifteen-year-old shouldn't have to share his room with his kid brother. So, ideally, four bedrooms. No apartments had four bedrooms.

That brought up the next item. Two full bathrooms, at least one and a half.

From there she added things she had enjoyed as Curtis's wife and lost in the transition to apartment living, mostly appliances.

Most of all, she wanted space and privacy. She wanted a house, plain and simple. Her mind sunk its hooks into the impossibilities, and she shook her head as if that would dislodge the worries. God would provide for her needs, if not her wants, something she couldn't even imagine yet. "And, Lord?" She looked at the ceiling, whispering. "My lease is up in three weeks."

Soft footfalls landed on Verity's ears and she straightened in her seat.

Des stood at the front of the hallway leading to the bedrooms. "Are you okay, Mom?"

"I'm fine. Better than fine, in fact." Verity stood. "I've been talking with God about getting us some more room."

Des brought her hands together underneath her chin and did a happy dance. "Are we going to move?"

"Yes," Verity said with authority. She just didn't know where. They shared a hopeful hug. "I love you, you know. You'll always be my little girl."

"Mom." Des's retort didn't contain the usual bite.

The doorbell rang. Garrett had arrived, two large bags with food from the pizza place in his hands. He leaned forward to kiss Verity on the cheek.

"Come on in, Garrett." Verity's voice wobbled on his name, and Des's smile turned to a flat line.

"I hope you're hungry. I refuse to take any of this home."

Des stayed in the kitchen, progress, even if the conversation felt forced.

The doorknob rattled a few minutes later. Keenan had come home early, and brought a guest.

Aunt Hazel stood on her doorstep. "I understand you are looking for a new home. I may have a solution."

Chapter 15

Verity glanced from Garrett to Keenan, as if wondering who had invited his aunt. Keenan stepped forward but Hazel spoke. "Don't blame the boy, Verity. I have a talent for worming things out of teenagers."

Garrett lifted his eyebrows and nodded his head.

Several emotions raced across Verity's face but she managed a calm response. "Come in, Hazel. I want to hear what my son's been telling you." The look she sent Keenan's way could have cut wood.

Garrett grabbed a couple of pizza slices while Verity settled with her guest. Should he stay in the background while they had their conversation? Not tonight. He'd expected to brainstorm solutions to the housing situation, but he welcomed Aunt Hazel's input.

Verity's wide-open eyes looked blank, her mind shutting out more information. He sat next to her on the couch and took her hand in his.

In her straightforward manner, Aunt Hazel said, "I had just about decided to sell my house. I'm getting too old for such a large place. I can't tell you how much Keenan has helped me." Aunt Hazel relaxed and leaned in closer. "Will you do me the favor of sharing my rattling old house?"

The offer surprised Garrett, but he prayed God would open Verity's mind to the possibility.

Verity said, "I can't possibly…"

"Before you say no, I think Aunt Hazel should look at this," Des interrupted. She handed her a piece of paper. "I found this on Mom's desk."

Verity gasped, but Aunt Hazel was already reading the page.

Aunt Hazel perched her glasses on her nose and studied the paper. When she finished, she laughed. "This looks like the list I put together when I was house hunting. When I hoped our home would be filled with all the children God would give us." She tapped Verity's knee. "You are blessed. God gave you three beautiful children before you lost your husband."

Verity paled. "I had forgotten you had lost your husband." In a low voice, she asked, "Why didn't you sell it back then?"

"I kept finding children to bring in. I had a dozen nieces and nephews, and I was a foster mother. But now my family, like Garrett here, is grown and my last foster child left last summer." She laughed. "Perhaps God emptied my house to make room for you."

Aunt Hazel made notes as she read the page. "Take a look."

Verity's hand shook as she read the paper. "This is impossible. That list was my Cinderella dream, everything I could imagine God giving me in a house."

"I'm sure there are more features you will find to your

liking. Because we serve that kind of God, not because my house is anything special."

Des held her hands to her mouth. "Does that mean I get my own room?"

Verity looked at Aunt Hazel, at Garrett, at Keenan—at Des. "Yes, and Mason, too."

"Hooray!" Mason jumped up and down.

Verity cringed, perhaps wondering if Aunt Hazel would change her mind.

Instead, the older woman smiled. "Please say yes."

Tears glittered in Verity's eyes as she said, "Yes. Yes!"

After the decision to move, they spent every spare hour of the month of March packing up everything in the apartment. Whenever Garrett arrived to help, Des disappeared to her room but at least she didn't lash out anymore.

Verity had more to pack than Garrett had expected. As small as their apartment was, she organized it well and kept things in order. "What will you do with your furniture?" Garrett asked. "You have some good pieces."

"Storage for now. It's not that expensive. I wish I could chop the bunk beds into kindling, but someone might need them in the future."

Throughout the month, they moved boxes every weekend. Verity wanted to have the bedrooms ready when they moved in, to make the transition easier on the children. "Mason doesn't remember any other home than that apartment. Poor kid." She put a battered train set on the shelf beside his bed. "He was crazy about trains when he was a toddler, and Curtis put that train together for him for our last Christmas together." When she rubbed the engine, her wedding ring flashed.

Garrett bit back his disappointment. The shadow of Verity's husband remained between them. Face it. She might never be ready for anyone else. His dreams might be as old and dusty as last year's Christmas decorations.

Aunt Hazel asked him about it one night, when they were alone. He said, "I wonder if it's too late for me. I tell myself God can work it out, if He wants it."

"Oh, I suspect He wants to. He keeps bringing you together. As long as she's under my roof, you don't need an excuse to stop by." His aunt's laughter tinkled like chimes. "God gives His children good gifts. She needs a good man, and you need a godly woman, strong enough to match you in passion and purpose." She patted his hand. "Don't worry about the children. They will come around." She handed him a box of photographs. "I ran across these when I was clearing out the bedrooms. Take a look."

Garrett left the pictures aside until the night before moving day. Aunt Hazel had collected pictures of the Sawtelle children, as well as some of the Reids, Finches and Tuttles. Verity appeared in several snaps. He hadn't realized how much Des looked like her mother. In the middle he found pictures from his football days.

He also found a picture of Verity, in her cheerleader's uniform, smiling, eyes flashing as she jumped under the Friday night football lights.

He knew just what he was going to do with it.

Verity sank into Hazel's comfortable bed, too exhausted to pay attention to the room, only to sleepily wonder where the mattress over her head had gone. She didn't stir until blazing morning light forced her to open her eyes.

Momentarily disoriented, she whispered, "Des?" Blinking several times, she came to full wakefulness. They had moved into the home of Garrett's aunt, a woman who'd adopted Keenan like a grandson she never had.

This morning Verity luxuriated in the details she had

overlooked the previous evening. The double bed looked like an ocean compared to the twin bunk. This mattress called for someone to share the space with her—a pet or even a husband. Heat flamed through her at the thought.

Verity didn't expect their stay would be permanent. Before then, she hoped to have debts paid off and maybe some money set aside for a new car or even a house.

Although she had seen the room before, with a few things left to unpack, something felt changed. Verity stood in the center, shut her eyes, picturing what she remembered of how the room used to look. As soon as she opened her eyes, she saw the difference. A photograph sat on the mantelpiece above an old fireplace. The girl in the Maple Notch green-and-gold cheerleader's uniform came from a different life. The future held limitless possibilities, especially when their team had won the state championship on the back of their talented and handsome star quarterback.

Someone knocked at her door, and Hazel entered when Verity said to come in. "I have breakfast started, if you're hungry."

"You don't need to do that," Verity said.

"I know. And I won't, not every day. But today I wanted to. How can you resist your own sister's muffins?" Hazel handed Verity a maple nut muffin, one of her favorites.

"Where did you get this picture? That was another world."

"No, just a different season." Hazel took the frame from Verity and stroked it gently. "But I'm not the one who put it here. Garrett must have done that."

Verity noticed a small envelope tucked into the corner of the frame. A bold, spiky, masculine hand had written her name on the envelope. Inside, it read, "To the prettiest girl at homecoming, then and now. Love, Garrett."

Her hand flew to her mouth, and her ring hit her upper

lip. She twisted it around. "I'll be downstairs before much longer." Should she wake the children? No, let them sleep.

When Verity combed her hair, her wedding ring got tangled in the snarls. She removed the ring, tugged away the loose hair. After staring at it for a long minute, she set it on her dresser. When she spread out her fingers, turning them over and over, they looked evenly matched, no adornment needed. Her fingers wrapped around the ring, covered it with a lace-edged linen hankie and placed it in her top drawer. Today was a new beginning, in more ways than one.

In the roomy kitchen the children were devouring food as if they hadn't eaten for a week. After pouring herself a cup of coffee, she joined them at the table. "Who's ready to finish unpacking today?" she asked, knowing how they would respond.

A simultaneous groan came from all three children, accompanied by Hazel's chuckle.

"I was just kidding. Mostly." Verity took another muffin and drank her coffee black, her ringless finger glowing as if her flesh had changed to gold, shades of King Midas. No one mentioned it. "Sometime today, get your rooms in order. You won't have much time when you get back to school tomorrow."

"I'm done." Mason jumped up. "Can I leave the table, Mom?"

Verity nodded.

"And I'm ready for the shower." Des stood without asking permission.

Verity opened her mouth, then closed it again. "Enjoy." They had two full bathrooms here. She had sunk into a luxurious bubble bath the night before, something she hadn't enjoyed for a long time. "Do you need a shower today?" she asked Keenan.

He sniffed his armpits—so like a boy—and shook his head. "I'll work on my room. Aaron asked me over this afternoon. Okay?"

Verity nodded. Hazel looked at the suddenly empty table. "I had forgotten what a whirlwind a house full of children is."

"Let me know if they're too rambunctious. I'll rein them in." She hoped.

They made it to church a few minutes before Sunday school, as usual. When she waved to Garrett, she wondered if he could see she wasn't wearing a ring. The pale line where the ring had been shone like a flashlight to her eyes.

Since several members of her Sunday school class had helped with the move, she brought tea shop muffins to share. In spite of the lively discussion, Verity kept checking her watch, eager for the class to end—to see Garrett during the worship service.

He slipped into the pew to her right as the congregation sang the first song. "How was your first night?" he whispered.

"Fine." Her heart beat quickly. She alternated between sticking her right hand out for him to see and hiding it behind her back.

When they sang one of her favorite praise songs, she gave herself to worship. When the lyrics talked about lifting up her hands, she raised her arms in praise.

Something had changed in Verity, but Garrett couldn't pin it down until they raised their arms and swayed with the music. No ring on her finger. He almost cried out loud, but instead he shut his eyes, bringing himself under control.

Garrett took verbatim notes of the sermon, forcing himself to listen instead of thinking about Verity. The pastor preached about following the right path, about knowing God's will. Ninety percent of anything they needed to know about how to live was already in the Bible but people let the other ten percent confuse them.

The sermon only confirmed Garrett's desire to take the next step forward with Verity. Once the crowd thinned, he approached the pastor. "I'm considering walking down the aisle with Verity. What do you think?" He held his breath, worried at his response.

The preacher clapped him on the back. "It's high time." He stared over Garrett's shoulder and pointed. "If you want to speak with her today, she's leaving."

"Thanks." Garrett pushed through the entrance doors and jogged to the car. Verity had the trunk up, putting away a few housewarming gifts people had given her. "Hey there."

"Garrett." Smiling, she tucked a stray hair behind her ear with her naked right hand.

"I see you took it off." He took a step closer.

Verity covered the offending hand with her left. "I did."

"Does that mean…? Can I ask…?"

"Yes." She smiled again. She took a step in his direction.

Garrett closed the distance between them and took Verity in his arms. When she looked into his eyes, her lips opened in invitation. He bent down and took one sweet kiss before he stepped back.

Her fingers touched her lips and his, a tentative smile welcoming the touch.

The car door opened. "Mom!" Des yelped.

Verity's back stiffened, but her grasp of Garrett's hand tightened. Turning with him to face the children, she said, "Des, this is my decision. Not yours or Keenan's or Mason's. The only Person to whom I am responsible is

God Himself." With a smile at Garrett, she said, "And, of course, Garrett."

Verity leaned forward, kissed Garrett again, soundly on the lips, before she dropped his hands. "Call me later."

"Yes. Of course. In five minutes."

Her laughter followed her as she climbed into her car. After Des turned a bewildered stare at Garrett, she climbed in her seat and shut the door.

He did call, an hour later. Throughout the week, he felt as lovesick as a teenager. He and Verity sent selfies everywhere they went and they texted whatever they were doing. Although they saw each other every day, they only had one evening together. He promised her a special date on Friday night.

On Thursday afternoon, Garrett stopped by the museum to check on Keenan's progress. To his surprise, Des was with her brother, her back turned to the door. She was arguing with him over a family tree. They spoke loud enough for him to hear.

"Doesn't it ever bother you? We know about Mom's family, back before the Revolutionary War. But we don't know anything about Dad's family."

"We know they were all in the military," Keenan said. "Grandpa Clark would know."

Des threw her hands in the air. "But we never see him."

"Have you tried emailing him?"

Des snorted. "Grandpa, on the computer? Don't make me laugh."

Garrett thought about leaving, but decided to stay. He couldn't avoid Des, not if he wanted things to work out with Verity. He stepped around the corner.

The kids continued their discussion, not even noticing his arrival. Amity motioned for him to come in. "I wasn't expecting you today."

Garrett grinned. "I bear good news."

"I'm glad to hear it. Keenan's doing fine, Garrett. I hope he continues working in the museum once he's off probation or whatever you call it."

Garrett placed Keenan's file folder on the table. "Before we call him in here, can you help Des research her father's family? She said a lot of them were in the military."

"Sure. Military records are fairly easy to research. She should be able to learn a lot of it online." After Amity entered names and dates into the computer, a half a dozen records sprang onto the screen. The search fascinated Garrett, and he followed leads for thirty minutes, before Amity called Des in.

The museum was empty. They walked from the dusty back rooms through the displays and offices. No sign of the kids.

"This isn't like Keenan," Amity said. She glanced at her watch. "Although technically his work hours were over." She patted Garrett on the shoulder. "I'm sure they're all right. They probably headed home."

Garrett said goodbye and took out his phone in his car. He started to text Verity, but decided against it. When he called to confirm their dinner plans, she didn't answer. He spruced up a bit and headed for Aunt Hazel's home.

A pale-faced Verity met him at the door dressed in her sweats. "Des didn't come home after school. She's gone somewhere, and Keenan is with her. Oh, Garrett." She melted into his arms.

Chapter 16

Verity stayed in Garrett's arms, his strength preparing her for the upcoming battle. When at last they stepped apart, his face looked as worry-worn as her own must. Hazel's and Mason's voices mingled from the direction of the living room.

"Have you heard from either Keenan or Des?" Garrett sat down on the lounge chair but leaned forward, both feet planted on the ground.

"Just this." Verity retrieved the message Keenan had sent.

It said, Garrett's eyes widened, surprised as she was, before he hit the return call button. No one answered. "I should tell you something."

"What?" she asked.

"I saw them both at the museum this afternoon. I don't think Des even knew I was there. She was working on her family tree, and wanted to know more about her father's family. Amity found some information on the web, but Des left before she could show it to her."

"I didn't know that." Verity rocked back and forth, worry splitting the seams of her calm. "Today I let Keenan take the car to work. What has he done?"

Garrett took her hands in his and prayed. His words reminded them that God was with them, and she relaxed.

But why hadn't Keenan called again? She dialed again, got another message that the line wasn't available. Because he was still driving, of course. She had warned him about using the phone while driving.

"A storm's brewing." Garrett pointed to the television. A late-winter storm was gathering from the northwest. According to the screen, the temperatures had dropped below freezing, with snow soon to follow.

Worst-case scenarios ran through Verity's head. A new driver, with zero experience driving in the snow. Accidents, injuries, no cell service…no way to call for help. Shutting her eyes didn't keep the dangerous scenarios from parading through her mind, and she trembled. Strong arms circled Verity, pulling her close. She buried her face in his shirt, allowing teardrops to fall.

Garrett held her, rubbing her back and hair. "God is watching over them. They'll be okay, you'll see." The way he said it, Verity almost believed it. The way he held her, she absorbed his strength, his care—dare she hope his love?

She pulled out of his embrace. "I'll be all right. But what do we do next?"

Garrett said, "Can either the phone or the car be tracked?"

Verity shook her head. "I'm not sure. I didn't set up the phone to track my kids. I never thought I'd need to." Her voice trailed away. "And the car doesn't have a GPS."

"Even if it did, the weather would probably block the signal anyway." He stood. "I'll fix us something to eat."

"I'm not hungry." The words came automatically.

"Doesn't matter. You will eat, even if it tastes like cardboard. You can't help your kids if your blood sugar is off and you run out of energy."

Her laughter was hollow. "I suppose you're right."

"Comfort food." He nodded, satisfied with himself. "Mason will be hungry before long even if we aren't."

"He likes chicken wings." How ridiculous her words sounded. She didn't have chicken wings in the freezer, didn't cook them herself. "He loves that horrible canned chicken noodle soup."

"I can do better than that." He pulled a bag of chicken chunks from the freezer, along with chicken stock. "Are there any veggies he won't eat?"

"He likes them, even spinach." The memory brought a faint smile.

"Good." He pulled out carrots and celery.

Verity grabbed some potatoes to peel. "I could have helped with the family tree. When Keenan was born, I wrote down everything Curtis knew about his family. I copied our family line, too, and stuck it in his baby book."

"Did you put the same information in Des's book?"

"Unfortunately, no." Keeping up with all those details had seemed less important than watching her baby girl's every movement. "Or she could always ask Amity. She's the expert."

"But Des wanted to explore Clark roots," Garrett said. "You have names, but how well do you know their stories?"

"Not all that well." Verity's eyes clouded. "Mostly I remember their stories about Curtis, cute stories that embarrass an adult."

The soup bubbled merrily but Verity couldn't relax. She

stood on the back door stoop, wind whipping under her sweatshirt, around her chest and arms. The sky darkened, almost black, too much for the time of day. "I can't stand just sitting here. I want to look for them."

"Eat first." Garrett dished out two bowls.

"Shouldn't we call Mason, Hazel…"

"We'll leave it for them."

Verity blew on the soup, cooling it enough to eat. The taste danced on her tongue as she gulped it down as quickly as she could. Without a word, Garrett refilled her bowl and she finished that. She felt more awake, energized. "Thanks. I needed that."

"I knew you did." Garrett rinsed off their bowls and put them in the dishwasher. "What else do we need to do before we head out?"

"Ask Hazel to take care of Mason."

Before Garrett could talk to his aunt, she came in the door. "I planned on staying with Mason, of course. You two go have some fun." She glanced at their faces, the empty soup bowls. "Something's happened."

"Des and Keenan are both gone, and we can't reach them by phone." Tears sparkled in Verity's eyes. "They're out there somewhere in this terrible weather."

Garrett's aunt appeared to have questions, but she kept quiet. "Do what you need to do. I'll be here by the phone in case they call."

"Let me tell Mason goodbye."

A sound asleep Mason lay on the couch, his hand resting on the floor. Verity brushed her lips across his cheeks and jerked back. "He feels hot. Too hot." Worry scattered shadowy pinpoints across her face.

"Mommy?" Mason sat up, rubbing his eyes. "I don't feel

so good." He coughed, surprising Garrett by how hoarse his voice and cough sounded.

"I'm going to check your temperature." Verity slipped past Garrett, heading for the bathroom.

Garrett sat on the couch next to Mason. "What's wrong, little guy?" He didn't know enough about children to know when something was critical, but he didn't look good.

"My chest hurts." Mason coughed again.

Verity's thermometer checked temperature by running over the forehead. Before Garrett could blink, she announced, "One hundred and two. Let me call the doctor." Verity pulled her phone out of her pocket and walked into the hallway.

"How does a bowl of chicken noodle soup sound?" Garrett helped Mason to his feet. "I made it especially for you."

Mason shook his head. "I just want to sleep." He lay back down and Garrett covered him with an afghan.

Aunt Hazel came in, a steaming bowl on a tray.

"You stole my idea. But he's sleeping," Garrett said.

"Poor boy." She pulled the afghan back from Mason's shoulder. "I brought you some soup. Think you can sit up for me?"

Garrett helped Mason into a sitting position, holding him against his side. Aunt Hazel spooned the broth into his mouth, until the bowl was empty. He lay back against the cushion.

Verity came from the kitchen, worry written on her face. "Did he eat anything?"

"A bowl of soup." Aunt Hazel beamed. "What did the doctor say?"

"To meet him at the hospital. But…"

Garrett gathered Verity's trembling form in his arms. The sky had fallen dark while they had eaten, and heavy spring snow filled the sky. He hated the thought of driving through the storm, dreaded the thought of a new driver like Keenan maneuvering the roads. He sent up a brief prayer and kissed the top of her head. "What do you want to do?"

"I have to take care of Mason." Her voice keened. "But what about Des? And Keenan? Why do I always have to choose one child over another?"

As much as Garrett wanted to stay with Verity, he didn't see how to make it happen. "I'll stay with Mason, get him to the doctor, while you look for Des and Keenan. Or the other way around. I hate the thought of you on the roads."

Arms akimbo, Aunt Hazel bristled. "And what about me? Both of you, go. I'll take Mason to the doctor. I've been with him since he got home from school, so I can tell them everything. He'll be fine." Her smile faded. "You'll be back before he even knows you're not here. I'm sure of it."

"I'll do whatever you need me to do." As much as Garrett wanted to give Verity advice, he kept quiet. Her eyes kept swinging from the snowstorm out the window to Mason's sleeping form.

She closed her eyes, her lips moving, as if in prayer. When she raised her eyes again, they had cleared. "I will come with you to find Des and Keenan. They matter, too."

"It's none of my business," Aunt Hazel said. "But I think you're making the right decision."

Verity gave Aunt Hazel her insurance card and other relevant information. "Let me get warm clothes for the kids. I doubt they were prepared for the storm." Verity ran upstairs.

While he was waiting, Garrett bundled Mason into Aunt Hazel's car. After she locked herself in the driver's seat, his aunt said, "I'll call you when I get him to the hospital. You take good care of that woman, promise me?"

"I promise." Garrett tugged his coat collar against the

merciless wind. His aunt's closet held a few scarves, hats, a mixture of unmatched mittens. He only found one extra blanket. Most of them probably covered beds for the new household members.

"I've got clothes for everyone." Verity added the items Garrett had brought into her bag. "Let's go."

They climbed into Garrett's SUV, their only choice since Keenan and Des had Verity's car. Grand theft auto crossed her mind, stories of parents who had their children arrested for taking the family car on a joyride. She couldn't imagine doing something like that.

Garrett glanced at her. "What's on your mind? Something has you frowning."

"The police." She shook her head. "I'd better file a missing-persons report, but whatever's up, I'm pretty sure he's only trying to help his sister."

Garrett nodded. The streets slid by without either one of them speaking until they passed a gas station. "Stop," she said.

The car skidded a few inches when he braked on the icy street, but no one was in the way. He pulled in front of the door. "What's up?"

"My gas tank was almost empty this morning. They'd need gas. And maybe to buy a map or ask directions or something." She was grasping at straws, but she prayed God would direct her to ask the right questions of the right people.

The first attendant hadn't seen the kids, the second had changed shifts since the estimated time of departure, but they found someone at the third gas station.

When the clerk saw their school pictures, he nodded. "Ayuh. They stopped by just before lunch. Asked me for a map of New York and New England." He grinned. "I wondered why they didn't just look it up online."

Because Verity had given them phones with the limited applications she could afford. Their phones weren't meant as aides for two teenage runaways.

They bought a map and went to the car. Garrett said, "Do you want to call the police?"

Verity shivered at the thought. Ever since Curtis had died, the sight of someone in uniform coming to her door left her uneasy. The police dedicated themselves to serve and protect, but she still felt that frisson of fear.

"We should report them missing," she admitted. "But before we get caught in answering their questions, I want to look at the map Keenan bought." Vermont, New Hampshire, Maine, Massachusetts, Connecticut. Of course.

Curtis's parents.

"I know where they're going."

Knowing the kids' destination removed a small slice of Verity's worry. But an inexperienced driver maneuvering slippery roads for much of the way was a recipe for disaster. Tree-lined roads were beautiful in summer and fall, as dangerous as the river Styx in the winter dark.

Her fingers fumbled as she searched her contacts for the Clarks' number. Since she rarely called, it was buried at the bottom of the list. Although they were nice enough, the frequent moves dictated by the military had kept them from growing close. After Curtis's death, they'd drifted farther apart. Now she realized her mistake—grandparents and grandchildren belonged to each other.

Verity's mother-in-law picked up on the first ring. "This is Alice Clark speaking."

Her tongue stuck to the roof of her mouth. "Alice, this is Verity." Before her mother-in-law could interrupt with good-to-hear-from-you noises, she plowed forward. "I know this sounds odd, but have you heard from either Keenan or Des today?"

Garrett looked at her, eyebrows raised.

"No?" Verity didn't know what to say, where to start.

"What's wrong, dear?" It hadn't taken much for Alice to pick up on Verity's distress.

Garrett made motions to hand him the phone. "My friend Garrett Sawtelle wants to speak with you." She handed it to him and listened to his side of the conversation.

Garrett pulled to the side of the road while he was on the phone. "Yes. They left about noon today...No, they didn't say where they were going...Des is working on a school project. She wants to know more about her father's family...Yes, I met him at the wedding. Verity and I went to high school together, though."

About the time Verity wondered how long the twenty questions would continue, Garrett wound it up. "If you hear from either of them, call us right away. You have Verity's phone number. My number is..." When he finished, he handed the phone to Verity. "They want to speak with you again." He rejoined the traffic headed south.

"Mr. Sawtelle sounds like a nice young man," Alice said. "I'm glad he's with you at a time like this. We'll call you if we hear anything." They said their goodbyes and disconnected.

"Are you ready to head south?" Garrett asked.

"As soon as we talk to the sheriff."

Chapter 17

While Verity made a missing-persons report, Garrett checked the map application on his phone. The Clarks lived in a small town near the Mattatuk State Forest, along the western boundary with New York. The app suggested three routes. The quickest drive ran through New Hampshire and south, along Highway 91.

Another route took them to the west, running through Vermont to New York and Connecticut. The third headed straight south. Garrett put himself in the place of the new sixteen-year-old driver. Keenan would want to get there quickly, and Verity agreed with Garrett's assessment. "He wants to get there as soon as possible. I bet he took the highway."

Once they reached the highway, weekend traffic crawled in both directions. Perhaps Keenan had avoided it by leaving earlier. Even so, a four- to five-hour trip was a major undertaking.

"What if Keenan is pulled over for speeding or something?" Verity stared at the side of the road. The snow had slowed to the point where Garrett turned off the windshield wipers every few minutes.

"At least he'd be safe. A cop might even suggest he call you."

The traffic slowed down more, due to an accident ahead.

"It's not them." He grabbed her hand for a moment with his right, keeping his left hand on the steering wheel. In spite of his reassurance, his heart worked overtime until they passed the vehicle—a truck, not Verity's car. He sent up a prayer for the people involved.

A weather report came over the radio, confirming what Garrett had already noticed. "The storm has eased, but expect more snow later."

Snowplows worked both sides of the highway. At least Keenan had started his trip before the storm began. If Keenan had taken this route, the pavement would be fairly safe.

The phone rang and Verity's hand slipped from Garrett's. She said, "It's Alice," as she punched the talk button.

They had reached the halfway point, and a diner welcomed them at the next exit. He could use a cup of coffee, and they might change plans after hearing from Alice.

"Keenan!" Verity's shriek was music to Garrett's ears.

Garrett made motions to go inside. After opening the door for Verity, he held her close while she continued talking without even taking a breath. He asked for two cups of coffee and a slice of blueberry pie for them to share.

After he placed the order, Verity took the phone away from her ear. "How much farther do we have to go?"

"We're about halfway there. Two hours if we're lucky, maybe as long as three."

Verity passed on the information. "No, I want to see you. Tonight."

Garrett thought he heard Des's voice on the other end.

"I understand you want to learn more about your father. But you can't just run away like this." Irritation was seeping back into Verity's voice. "We'll talk about it when we get there. Yes, Garrett is with me."

Garrett's ears perked up, expecting an explosion from the other end. Instead, the conversation continued. "No. Don't go anywhere until we arrive at your grandparents' house." More conversation followed.

The server brought their coffee and pie, as well as a small pitcher of cream with an assortment of sugar and sweeteners. Garrett fixed her coffee, with a smidgeon of cream.

"Goodbye, Alice. I'm glad they're with you, and safe." At last the phone call ended. Verity took a long swallow of the coffee, its warmth spreading from head to toes. "I needed that. Thank you." She took over the pie. After a tentative first bite, she took a second and finished the slice before she noticed the empty space in front of Garrett.

In spite of everything that had happened that night, Garrett couldn't help laughing. He signaled the server. She topped up their coffees. "I'll take another slice of pie, please."

Verity turned bright red. "I apologize."

"No problem." He laughed again, harder this time. "Blame it on relief that the kids are safe. I was sitting here thinking I know how much you love blueberry pie and coffee with a touch of cream. I am more to you than a friend, and you know it."

Her eyes danced. "Not to mention the fact you're driving me through three states to look for my kids. You're my friend, my support—the kind of man my kids need for a father."

That you want for a husband? "Whether or not they agree?"

She reached across the table and curled her fingers around his. "Whether or not they agree. Yes."

The warmth from the hot coffee wrapped Verity in a cocoon with Garrett, spun out of the love she allowed herself to admit.

When the server brought the check, the warm feeling disappeared. Snow had started falling again. With the slippery roads, they might not make it to the Clarks' until close to midnight. And what was happening with Mason?

Heavy, thick snow hit her in the face before they left the awning. Garrett squinted into the sky, his baseball cap not providing any protection. "The storm has blown back our way," he said.

"We stayed inside too long." Verity's heart fought the guilt that threatened to swamp her.

"We'll get there," Garrett growled. He refilled the tank, and the car slipped on its way out of the parking lot.

Lord, keep us safe. Verity took comfort in knowing that Keenan and Des had arrived in Connecticut and were off the roads.

The phone rang—Hazel was calling. "How's Mason?" Verity asked.

"The doctor wants to keep him overnight. He says not to worry, he just wants to keep an eye on him." Hazel paused for a breath. "He promised to call you if anything changes."

"That's good, I guess." They chatted a few moments more and disconnected. Verity shared the news with Garrett.

The traffic was much lighter now, and Garrett found a

spot behind a snowplow. Although they moved at turtle speed, they didn't have to worry about spinning out of control. Verity kept quoting the psalm "What time I am afraid, I will trust in Thee." At the next exit, the plow left the highway. Caution lights warned against traveling in the storm. Thirty-five minutes and one exit later, Garrett said, "We have to get off the road."

Verity agreed. With the hour creeping past eleven, the exhaustion evident in Garrett's posture pushed them both into danger. The first hotel they pulled into had two rooms available, reasonably priced but still an unexpected expense. Because of Hazel's generosity, Verity had a little more wiggle room in her budget, enough to pay for the night.

With all the clothes Verity had brought for the children, she had forgotten to pack anything for herself. Garrett followed her down the hall, until they reached their side-by-side rooms. "Rest well, sweetheart." He pushed a tendril of hair back from her face and kissed her lips.

Verity rested her head against the door for a moment before entering. After a call to Alice, alerting her to their change of plans, she climbed into bed, and slept for a solid six hours.

Loud knocking on the door awoke her at half-past five. The desk clerk stood at her door, a serving table in front of him. "Mr. Sawtelle ordered breakfast for you, ma'am."

The smells—crisp bacon, perfectly fried eggs, fresh baked goods—reminded Verity how hungry she was. She made herself eat slowly, to get the most benefit of the food. After a quick hop in the shower, she climbed into her clothes from last night. The weather report said the storm had ended but cautioned travelers.

Garrett knocked a few minutes after six, while she was

drying her hair. He looked better than he had any right to be after the night they'd had.

"I'm almost ready." She gestured for him to come in. "Let me finish drying my hair." The air outside was cold enough to freeze wet hair into icicles. Finished, she made sure no stray curls escaped her wool cap. "Now I'm ready."

A few minutes later they were on the road. Towers of snow rose on both sides of the highway, the kind of heavy spring storm New England experienced from time to time. "I thought Connecticut escaped heavy snow like this."

"We haven't reached Connecticut yet." Garrett pointed to a sign ahead. "There's the state line and a welcome center a mile or so past that."

To Verity's surprise, Garrett pulled into the welcome center, to check on the best route to the Clarks' hometown. "They say to stay on the highway until we get closer. The back roads won't be as well plowed after the snow. And we don't have time to stop by the woods on a snowy evening."

Verity giggled at the reference to Robert Frost's poem.

"But the house we want is in a village and I hope to arrive before the day gets under way."

Verity pulled out the phone, wondering if she should call yet. Seven-fifteen. Even if they weren't awake, she should call. She explained the situation. "We expect to be there in an hour, an hour and a half, tops."

Keenan got on the phone. "We have something we've got to do before we leave. We may not be at the house when you get here but you don't have to worry." He wouldn't explain and hung up after saying goodbye.

"What's up?" Garrett asked.

"He's taking Des someplace else and he wouldn't tell me where." Verity's voice escalated, and she told herself to calm down.

"Call Mrs. Clark," Garrett said.

Of course. She hit the speed-dial number she had added earlier. "Alice, Keenan says he's going somewhere else. Please don't let them leave."

"They're going to Curtis's grave," Alice whispered, as though cupping her hand over the phone. "You haven't been back there since the memorial day, two years ago. Before Mason got sick."

Alice must have said something that made Verity shrivel inside. The confidence and backbone she had worked so hard to acquire thinned, leaving her vulnerable. Garrett prayed for her to remain strong.

Every few seconds, he glanced at her. Color filled her face, her back straightened, her legs stretched in front of her, the phone held tightly to her ear. "That's fine. But whatever you do, don't let them go the cemetery alone." She stuffed the phone into her purse with an angry shove.

"Curtis's grave?" Garrett asked.

Verity nodded. "I'm hoping Alice will go with them. Who knows where they'll end up if they're alone?"

"No telling." He pointed to a road sign. "That's our exit, fifteen miles ahead. Do you know the way to the cemetery?"

"I think so, although it will look different in the snow." She stared at the roadside as they passed. "We came down here several times the first two years. Curtis and I hadn't bought burial plots—never expected to need them so soon, since we were young. So he was buried here, next to the plots his parents had purchased."

She closed her eyes, her hands dancing in her lap as if she were drawing a picture. "I can get us there."

When they pulled into the freshly plowed parking lot, another car sat near the entrance, with an older couple inside. "Curtis's parents?" Garrett asked.

Verity nodded. She bent forward, peering through the windshield. "And there's Keenan and Des. Let's go."

At her invitation, Garrett's heart warmed. Nevertheless, cold air slapped his face when he opened the door.

Verity folded back the hood of her parka and walked straight for the Clarks' car. Alice opened the window on the passenger's side. "Hi, Alice. Curt."

The Clarks waved back. Verity gestured for Garrett to come closer. "This is our family friend, Garrett Sawtelle."

"Garrett, good to meet you. Keenan has told us some wonderful things about you. Des…"

"Des isn't used to the idea of Verity having another man in her life," Garrett said.

Alice and Curtis didn't look too happy about the idea, either, but were too polite to say so. Verity's eyes fixed on her children, who were kneeling in the snow by their father's grave. Their footprints showed their struggle through the snow, knee-deep in some places.

Verity left them alone but stood by the car, ready to move if they asked for her. After a couple of minutes, Keenan noticed her and waved. He spoke to Des, but she shook her head.

"You can wait in the car where it's warm," Verity told Garrett.

"I spent half the night in the car. I need to stretch my legs." Also, he wanted to stand by Verity's side, in case she needed him. "It's not that cold." As the sun rose toward midday, the temperature increased, above freezing at least, not so uncomfortable.

Des looked at Verity and beckoned her forward. Verity turned to Garrett. "Will you come with me?" She extended her hand, and he took it.

In this place, at this time, she was making a statement

to her children. *Lord, if we're making the wrong decision, let us know. Soon.*

The boot prints ended after a few feet. One of them, probably Keenan, had cleared the snow wide enough to walk. The grave was at the far end of the row, making it easier to cross the quiet grave sites. The space in front of the tombstone was cleared. The simple cross and dates of service reminded anyone who saw it of the departed's sacrifice for his country.

Curtis Clark had been so much more than a soldier. Two children had risked a bad storm and their mother's fury to pay him honor. If Garrett died now, who would mourn his passing? He must pale by comparison to their hero father. Even Verity might doubt him.

Tears spilled down Verity's cheeks. He wondered if she would change her mind, let him go, but, if anything, her fingers tightened on his. Both children looked at them, solemn-faced, Des's tear-streaked. No one appeared angry. *Lord, make it so!*

Without warning, Verity and Des ran toward each other, wrapped in a hug and then moved to the grave, including Keenan in the hug. While the three of them laughed and cried, not a scolding word was heard.

Together, the three of them left the grave and headed in his direction. He prepared to fade away, to wait for them in his car, but his feet wouldn't move. This family had taken root in his heart. This was the woman he loved, the children he wanted to help raise.

With her arms wrapped around her children, Verity stopped in front of Garrett. His hand fell on Verity's shoulder, where it should be, and she shifted closer to Des, making room. He took his place at her side. The four of them looked at one another without speaking.

The kids took a few steps away, whispering to each other. When they rejoined Verity and Garrett, Des said, "I had to say goodbye to Daddy. I had to learn more about him. He'll always be with me. I'm a Clark. I know he loved me, and I love him. But I told him something else, as well."

She pulled Garrett close and whispered in his ear. Second by second, Garrett's grin grew from almost a frown to a face-wide smile. She stepped back, making space for him.

Warmth bloomed in Verity's chest when Garrett took her hand, where both children could see. He peeled back the glove, until her fingers appeared. He rubbed her finger, newly ringless, and smiled. "Des told me—" Garrett looked at the girl, as if unable to believe what she had said "—she told her father that she thinks she'll have a new father soon."

Verity's left hand flew to her lips. She felt unable to speak, or take a breath.

"I would be honored to be a father to both of you and Mason. Although I know I can never take Curtis's place." Garrett waited.

"Yes!" Keenan punched his fist into the air, and Des offered a shy smile.

Garrett turned his attention back to Verity. "When we talked about this last night, I never imagined God would answer our prayers so…enthusiastically. Abundantly. Quickly." Still holding on to Verity's hand, Garrett went down on one knee. "With the blessing of your children, and the approval of God above, will you take me as your husband, your partner, the father of your children?"

"Yes." Verity knelt by Garrett in the snow and kissed him, fully, on the lips.

"Snow angels!" Keenan shouted.

"Only if you join us." Verity matched the gleam in Garrett's eyes. They lay on their backs and made angels in the snow.

The children flopped beside them, capturing all four points of the compass in a circle of angels. Garrett turned toward Verity and sealed their love with a kiss.

* * * * *

REQUEST YOUR FREE BOOKS!

2 FREE INSPIRATIONAL NOVELS
PLUS 2
FREE
MYSTERY GIFTS

Love Inspired®

YES! Please send me 2 FREE Love Inspired® novels and my 2 FREE mystery gifts (gifts are worth about $10). After receiving them, if I don't wish to receive any more books, I can return the shipping statement marked "cancel." If I don't cancel, I will receive 6 brand-new novels every month and be billed just $4.99 per book in the U.S. or $5.49 per book in Canada. That's a saving of at least 17% off the cover price. It's quite a bargain! Shipping and handling is just 50¢ per book in the U.S. and 75¢ per book in Canada.* I understand that accepting the 2 free books and gifts places me under no obligation to buy anything. I can always return a shipment and cancel at any time. Even if I never buy another book, the two free books and gifts are mine to keep forever.

105/305 IDN GH5P

Name _____ (PLEASE PRINT) _____

Address _____ Apt. # _____

City _____ State/Prov. _____ Zip/Postal Code _____

Signature (if under 18, a parent or guardian must sign)

Mail to the **Reader Service**:
IN U.S.A.: P.O. Box 1867, Buffalo, NY 14240-1867
IN CANADA: P.O. Box 609, Fort Erie, Ontario L2A 5X3

**Are you a subscriber to Love Inspired® books
and want to receive the larger-print edition?
Call 1-800-873-8635 or visit www.ReaderService.com.**

* Terms and prices subject to change without notice. Prices do not include applicable taxes. Sales tax applicable in N.Y. Canadian residents will be charged applicable taxes. Offer not valid in Quebec. This offer is limited to one order per household. Not valid for current subscribers to Love Inspired books. All orders subject to credit approval. Credit or debit balances in a customer's account(s) may be offset by any other outstanding balance owed by or to the customer. Please allow 4 to 6 weeks for delivery. Offer available while quantities last.

Your Privacy—The Reader Service is committed to protecting your privacy. Our Privacy Policy is available online at www.ReaderService.com or upon request from the Reader Service.

We make a portion of our mailing list available to reputable third parties that offer products we believe may interest you. If you prefer that we not exchange your name with third parties, or if you wish to clarify or modify your communication preferences, please visit us at www.ReaderService.com/consumerchoice or write to us at Reader Service Preference Service, P.O. Box 9062, Buffalo, NY 14240-9062. Include your complete name and address.

LI15

REQUEST YOUR FREE BOOKS!

2 FREE INSPIRATIONAL NOVELS
PLUS 2 *FREE* MYSTERY GIFTS

Love Inspired® HISTORICAL

YES! Please send me 2 FREE Love Inspired® Historical novels and my 2 FREE mystery gifts (gifts are worth about $10). After receiving them, if I don't wish to receive any more books, I can return the shipping statement marked "cancel." If I don't cancel, I will receive 4 brand-new novels every month and be billed just $4.99 per book in the U.S. or $5.49 per book in Canada. That's a saving of at least 17% off the cover price. It's quite a bargain! Shipping and handling is just 50¢ per book in the U.S. and 75¢ per book in Canada.* I understand that accepting the 2 free books and gifts places me under no obligation to buy anything. I can always return a shipment and cancel at any time. Even if I never buy another book, the two free books and gifts are mine to keep forever.

102/302 IDN GH6Z

Name	(PLEASE PRINT)	
Address		Apt. #
City	State/Prov.	Zip/Postal Code

Signature (if under 18, a parent or guardian must sign)

Mail to the **Reader Service:**
IN U.S.A.: P.O. Box 1867, Buffalo, NY 14240-1867
IN CANADA: P.O. Box 609, Fort Erie, Ontario L2A 5X3

Want to try two free books from another series?
Call 1-800-873-8635 or visit www.ReaderService.com.

* Terms and prices subject to change without notice. Prices do not include applicable taxes. Sales tax applicable in N.Y. Canadian residents will be charged applicable taxes. Offer not valid in Quebec. This offer is limited to one order per household. Not valid for current subscribers to Love Inspired Historical books. All orders subject to credit approval. Credit or debit balances in a customer's account(s) may be offset by any other outstanding balance owed by or to the customer. Please allow 4 to 6 weeks for delivery. Offer available while quantities last.

Your Privacy—The Reader Service is committed to protecting your privacy. Our Privacy Policy is available online at www.ReaderService.com or upon request from the Reader Service.

We make a portion of our mailing list available to reputable third parties that offer products we believe may interest you. If you prefer that we not exchange your name with third parties, or if you wish to clarify or modify your communication preferences, please visit us at www.ReaderService.com/consumerschoice or write to us at Reader Service Preference Service, P.O. Box 9062, Buffalo, NY 14240-9062. Include your complete name and address.

LIH15